THE GHOST

THE GHOST

A FANTASIA ON MODERN THEMES

Arnold Bennett

NONSUCH

First published 1907
Copyright © in this edition Nonsuch Publishing, 2007

Nonsuch Publishing
Cirencester Road, Chalford, Stroud, Gloucestershire, GL6 8PE

Nonsuch Publishing (Ireland)
73 Lower Leeson Street, Dublin 2, Ireland

www.nonsuch-publishing.com

Nonsuch Publishing is an imprint of NPI Media Group

For comments or suggestions, please email the editor of this series at:
classics@tempus-publishing.com

British Library Cataloguing in Publication Data.
A catalogue record for this book is available from the British Library.

ISBN 978 1 84588 383 6

Typesetting and origination by NPI Media Group
Printed in Great Britain

CONTENTS

INTRODUCTION TO THE MODERN EDITION

ARNOLD BENNETT WAS BORN ABOVE a pawnbroker's shop in Hanley, Staffordshire, in 1867. He grew up in what was then a rather grim industrial region of the West Midlands, dominated by the manufacture of crockery, for which it became known as the 'Potteries.' From these provincial roots he went on to become a world-famous novelist, living much of his adult life in the cosmopolitan surroundings of London and Paris, but never forgetting the debt he owed to his birthplace for giving him the setting for so many of his novels, and for inspiring him to write so evocatively that he was credited with bringing European Realism to the English novel.

After a childhood spent in the comfortable prosperity that grew from his father's successful career as a solicitor, as a young man Arnold Bennett uprooted himself and moved to London in 1889. Here he took a position as a clerk in a solicitor's office, but, assured in his intention not to follow in his father's footsteps, he began to pursue a career as a writer. His new surroundings provided the ideal environment for this, as he was soon introduced to a circle of writers who recognised his abilities and encouraged his literary aspirations. Before long he had taken up journalism full-time, and became the assistant editor of *Woman* magazine. He subsequently became its editor, reviewing books and writing articles on an array of subjects, something he was to continue to do throughout his life, and he steadily acquired a reputation as a respected London journalist.

Within a few years he had published his first novel, *A Man from the North* (1898), quickly followed by *Anna of the Five Towns* (1902). Both works received critical acclaim, and *Anna* became the first of a succession of novels that detailed life in the Potteries region of his birth, set in fictionalised versions of real locations found in and around the area today known as Stoke-on-Trent, which he referred to as the 'Five Towns'. These novels are regarded as making significant contributions to the English Realist tradition, in particular *The Old Wives' Tale* (1908) and *Clayhanger* (1910), both of which are highly demonstrative of one of the most dominant influences upon Bennett, that of the French Realists such as Flaubert and Balzac. This influence is evident in many ways: writing that is rich in observation and atmosphere, stories that are filled with perceptive descriptions of people and places, and settings that portray the specific political and cultural make-up of this industrial pocket of England as it was at the end of the Victorian Age. These works are particularly powerful in their studies of ordinary individuals in conflict with their environment, circumstances and families, an ability which indicates Bennett's acute attention to the nuances of everyday life in the places he was depicting.

Despite the strong association with the Potteries of his birth, Arnold Bennett's abilities were not limited to this genre alone. His life and experiences in London, and later Paris, where he lived between 1903 and 1911, inspired in him a different kind of output, and he produced a number of more sensational and entertaining works, often referred to as his 'fantasias on modern themes.' These, which include *The Grand Babylon Hotel* (1902), *The Ghost* (1907), *The Card* (1911) and *Imperial Palace* (1930), were very popular in their day, and provided the basis for several successful dramatisations. They demonstrate his interest in exploring the opulence and luxury that existed in the world, something which provides a direct contrast to the provincial drudgery he portrayed in the 'Five Towns' works, but which fascinated him in equal measure. He continued to produce novels of the highest quality throughout the 1920s and '30s; works such as *Riceyman Steps,* which was set wholly in London and conveys the unglamorous setting of the Clerkenwell district with as much skill and impact as any of the Potteries novels. This portrait of a miserly London bookseller was widely praised on its publication in 1923.

By the time he reached his later years, Arnold Bennett had become a celebrated figure on the London literary scene, with a body of work which included short stories, essays, reviews and plays, as well as his posthumously published journals, which were hugely popular in their day. He was one of the few writers recruited by the government to assist in the production of war propaganda in 1914, and he became influential within the organisations created to this end, visiting the front lines and writing pamphlets to encourage young men to enlist. His status as a literary icon of his time is undoubted, and the offer of a knighthood, which he declined, is testament to this. He died from typhoid in 1931 and his ashes are buried in the cemetery at Burslem, one of the six towns of the Potteries.

I

MY SPLENDID COUSIN

I AM EIGHT YEARS OLDER now. It had never occurred to me that I am advancing in life and experience until, in setting myself to recall the various details of the affair, I suddenly remembered my timid confusion before the haughty mien of the clerk at Keith Prowse's.

I had asked him:

"Have you any amphitheatre seats for the Opera to-night?"

He did not reply. He merely put his lips together and waved his hand slowly from side to side.

Not perceiving, in my simplicity, that he was thus expressing a sublime pity for the ignorance which my demand implied, I innocently proceeded:

"Nor balcony?"

This time he condescended to speak.

"Noth—ing, sir."

Then I understood that what he meant was: "Poor fool! why don't you ask for the moon?"

I blushed. Yes, I blushed before the clerk at Keith Prowse's, and turned to leave the shop. I suppose he thought that as a Christian it was his duty to enlighten my pitiable darkness.

"It's the first Rosa night to-night," he said with august affability. "I had a couple of stalls this morning, but I've just sold them over the telephone for six pound ten."

He smiled. His smile crushed me. I know better now. I know that clerks in box-offices, with their correct neckties and their air of continually doing wonders over the telephone, are not, after all, the grand masters of the operatic world. I know that that manner of theirs is merely a part of their attire, like their cravats; that they are not really responsible for the popularity of great sopranos; and that they probably go home at nights to Fulham by the white omnibus, or to Hammersmith by the red one—and not in broughams.

"I see," I observed, carrying my crushed remains out into the street. Impossible to conceal the fact that I had recently arrived from Edinburgh as raw as a ploughboy!

If you had seen me standing irresolute on the pavement, tapping my stick of Irish bog-oak idly against the kerbstone, you would have seen a slim youth, rather nattily dressed (I think), with a shadow of brown on his upper lip, and a curl escaping from under his hat, and the hat just a little towards the back of his head, and a pretty good chin, and the pride of life in his ingenuous eye. Quite unaware that he was immature! Quite unaware that the supple curves of his limbs had an almost feminine grace that made older fellows feel paternal! Quite unaware that he had everything to learn, and that all his troubles lay before him! Actually fancying himself a man because he had just taken his medical degree …

The June sun shone gently radiant in a blue sky, and above the roofs milky-bosomed clouds were floating in a light wind. The town was bright, fresh, alert, as London can be during the season, and the joyousness of the busy streets echoed the joyousness of my heart (for I had already, with the elasticity of my years, recovered from the reverse inflicted on me by Keith Prowse's clerk). On the opposite side of the street were the rich premises of a well-known theatrical club, whose weekly entertainments had recently acquired fame. I was, I recollect, proud of knowing the identity of the building—it was one of the few things I did know in London—and I was observing with interest the wondrous livery of the two menials motionless behind the glass of its portals, when a tandem equipage drew up in front of the pile, and the menials darted out, in their white gloves, to prove that they were alive and to justify their existence.

It was an amazingly complete turnout, and it well deserved all the attention it attracted, which was considerable. The horses were capricious, highly polished greys, perhaps a trifle undersized, but with such an action as is not to be bought for less than twenty-five guineas a hoof; the harness was silver-mounted; the dog-cart itself a creation of beauty and nice poise; the groom a pink and priceless perfection. But the crown and summit of the work was the driver—a youngish gentleman who, from the gloss of his peculiarly shaped collar to the buttons of his diminutive boots, exuded an atmosphere of expense. His gloves, his scarf-pin, his watch-chain, his moustache, his eye-glass, the crease in his nether garments, the cut of his coat-tails, the curves of his hat—all uttered with one accord the final word of fashion, left nothing else to be said. The correctness of Keith Prowse's clerk was as naught to his correctness. He looked as if he had emerged immaculate from the outfitter's boudoir, an achievement, the pride of Bond Street.

As this marvellous creature stood up and prepared to alight from the vehicle, he chanced to turn his eye-glass in my direction. He scanned me carelessly, glanced away, and scanned me again with a less detached stare. And I, on my part, felt the awakening of a memory.

"That's my cousin Sullivan," I said to myself. "I wonder if he wants to be friends."

Our eyes coquetted. I put one foot into the roadway, withdrew it, restored it to the roadway, and then crossed the street.

It was indeed the celebrated Sullivan Smith, composer of those so successful musical comedies, *The Japanese Cat*, *The Arabian Girl*, and *My Queen*. And he condescended to recognize me! His gestures indicated, in fact, a warm desire to be cousinly. I reached him. The moment was historic. While the groom held the wheeler's head, and the twin menials assisted with dignified inactivity, we shook hands.

"How long is it?" he said.

"Fifteen years—about," I answered, feeling deliciously old.

"Remember I punched your head?"

"Rather!" (Somehow I was proud that he had punched my head.)

"No credit to me," he added magnanimously, "seeing I was years older than you and a foot or so taller. By the way, Carl, *how* old did you say you were?"

He regarded me as a sixth-form boy might regard a fourth-form boy.

"I didn't say I was any age," I replied. "But I'm twenty-three."

"Well, then, you're quite old enough to have a drink. Come into the club and partake of a gin-and-angostura, old man. I'll clear all this away."

He pointed to the equipage, the horses, and the groom, and with an apparently magic word whispered into the groom's ear he did in fact clear them away. They rattled and jingled off in the direction of Leicester Square, while Sullivan muttered observations on the groom's driving.

"Don't imagine I make a practice of tooling tandems down to my club," said Sullivan. "I don't. I brought the thing along to-day because I've sold it complete to Lottie Cass. You know her, of course?"

"I don't."

"Well, anyhow," he went on after this check, "I've sold her the entire bag of tricks. What do you think I'm going to buy?"

"What?"

"A motor-car, old man!"

In those days the person who bought a motor-car was deemed a fearless adventurer of romantic tendencies. And Sullivan so deemed himself. The very word "motor-car" then had a strange and thrilling romantic sound with it.

"The deuce you are!" I exclaimed.

"I am," said he, happy in having impressed me. He took my arm as though we had been intimate for a thousand years, and led me fearlessly past the swelling menials within the gate to the club smoking-room, and put me into a grandfather's chair of pale heliotrope plush in front of an onyx table, and put himself into another grandfather's chair of heliotrope plush. And in the cushioned quietude of the smoking-room, where light-shod acolytes served gin-and-angostura as if serving gin-and-angostura had been a religious rite, Sullivan went through an extraordinary process of unchaining himself. His form seemed to be crossed and re-crossed with chains—gold chains. At the end of one gold chain was a gold cigarette-case, from which he produced gold-tipped cigarettes. At the end of another was a gold matchbox. At the end of another, which he may or may not have drawn out by mistake, were all sorts of things—knives, keys, mirrors, and pencils. A singular ceremony! But I was now in the world of gold.

And then smoke ascended from the gold-tipped cigarettes as incense from censers, and Sullivan lifted his tinted glass of gin-and-angostura, and I, perceiving that such actions were expected of one in a theatrical club, responsively lifted mine, and the glasses collided, and Sullivan said:

"Here's to the end of the great family quarrel."

"I'm with you," said I.

And we sipped.

My father had quarrelled with his mother in an epoch when even musical comedies were unknown, and the quarrel had spread, as family quarrels do, like a fire or the measles. The punching of my head by Sullivan in the extinct past had been one of its earliest consequences.

"May the earth lie lightly on them!" said Sullivan.

He was referring to the originators of the altercation. The tone in which he uttered this wish pleased me—it was so gentle. It hinted that there was more in Sullivan than met the eye, though a great deal met the eye. I liked him. He awed me, and he also seemed to me somewhat ridiculous in his excessive pomp. But I liked him.

The next instant we were talking about Sullivan Smith. How he contrived to switch the conversation suddenly into that channel I cannot imagine. Some people have a gift of conjuring with conversations. They are almost always frankly and openly interested in themselves, as Sullivan was interested in himself. You may seek to foil them; you may even violently wrench the conversation into other directions. But every effort will be useless. They will beat you. You had much better lean back in your chair and enjoy their legerdemain.

In about two minutes Sullivan was in the very midst of his career.

"I never went in for high art, you know. All rot! I found I could write melodies that people liked and remembered." (He was so used to reading interviews with himself in popular weeklies that he had caught the formalistic phraseology, and he was ready apparently to mistake even his cousin for an interviewer. But I liked him.) "And I could get rather classy effects out of an orchestra. And so I kept on. I didn't try to be Wagner. I just stuck to Sullivan Smith. And, my boy, let me tell you it's only five years since *The Japanese Cat* was produced, and I'm only twenty-seven, my boy! And now, who is there that doesn't know me?" He put his elbows on the onyx. "Privately, between cousins, you know, I made seven thousand quid last year, and spent half that. I live on half my income; always have done; always shall. Good principle! I'm a man of business, I am, Carl Foster. Give the public what they want, and save half your income—that's the ticket. Look at me. I've got to act the duke; it pays, so I do it. I *am* a duke. I get twopence apiece royalty on my photographs. That's what you'll never reach up to, not if you're the biggest doctor in the world." He laughed. "By the way, how's Jem getting along? Still practising at Totnes?"

"Yes," I said.

"Doing well?"

"Oh! So—so! You see, we haven't got seven thousand a year, but we've got five hundred each, and Jem's more interested in hunting than in doctoring. He wants me to go into partnership with him. But I don't see myself."

"Ambitious, eh, like I was? Got your degree in Edinburgh?"

I nodded, but modestly disclaimed being ambitious like he was.

"And your sister Lilian?"

"She's keeping house for Jem."

"Pretty girl, isn't she?"

"Yes," I said doubtfully. "Sings well, too."

"So you cultivate music down there?"

"Rather!" I said. "That is, Lilian does, and I do when I'm with her.

We're pretty mad on it. I was dead set on hearing Rosetta Rosa in *Lohengrin* to-night, but there isn't a seat to be had. I suppose I shall push myself into the gallery."

"No, you won't," Sullivan put in sharply. "I've got a box. There'll be a chair for you. You'll see my wife. I should never have dreamt of going. Wagner bores me, though I must say I've got a few tips from him. But when we heard what a rush there was for seats Emmeline thought we ought to go, and I never cross her if I can help it. I made Smart give us a box."

"I shall be delighted to come," I said. "There's only one Smart, I suppose? You mean Sir Cyril?"

"The same, my boy. Lessee of the Opera, lessee of the Diana, lessee of the Folly, lessee of the Ottoman. If anyone knows the colour of his cheques I reckon it's me. He made me—that I will say; but I made him, too. Queer fellow! Awfully cute of him to get elected to the County Council. It was through him I met my wife. Did you ever see Emmeline when she was Sissie Vox?"

"I'm afraid I didn't."

"You missed a treat, old man. There was no one to touch her in boys' parts in burlesque. A dashed fine woman she is—though I say it, dashed fine!" He seemed to reflect a moment. "She's a spiritualist. I wish she wasn't. Spiritualism gets on her nerves. I've no use for it myself, but it's her life. It gives her fancies. She got some sort of a silly notion—don't tell her I said this, Carlie—about Rosetta Rosa. Says she's unlucky—Rosa, I mean. Wanted me to warn Smart against engaging her. *Me!* Imagine it! Why, Rosa will be the making of this opera season! She's getting a terrific salary, Smart told me."

"It's awfully decent of you to offer me a seat," I began to thank him.

"Stuff!" he said. "Cost me nothing." A clock struck softly. "Christopher! it's half-past twelve, and I'm due at the Diana at twelve. We're rehearsing, you know."

We went out of the club arm in arm, Sullivan toying with his eye-glass.

"Well, you'll toddle round to-night, eh? Just ask for my box. You'll find they'll look after you. So long!"

He walked off.

"I say," he cried, returning hastily on his steps, and lowering his voice, "when you meet my wife, don't say anything about her theatrical career. She don't like it. She's a great lady now. See?"

"Why, of course!" I agreed.

He slapped me on the back and departed.

It is easy to laugh at Sullivan. I could see that even then—perhaps more clearly then than now. But I insist that he was lovable. He had little directly to do with my immense adventure, but without him it could not have happened. And so I place him in the forefront of the narrative.

II

AT THE OPERA

IT WAS WITH A CERTAIN nervousness that I mentioned Sullivan's name to the gentleman at the receipt of tickets—a sort of transcendantly fine version of Keith Prowse's clerk—but Sullivan had not exaggerated his own importance. They did look after me. They looked after me with such respectful diligence that I might have been excused for supposing that they had mistaken me for the Shah of Persia in disguise. I was introduced into Sullivan's box with every circumstance of pomp. The box was empty. Naturally I had arrived there first. I sat down, and watched the enormous house fill, but not until I had glanced into the mirror that hung on the crimson partition of the box to make sure that my appearance did no discredit to Sullivan and the great lady, his wife.

At eight o'clock, when the conductor appeared at his desk to an accompaniment of applauding taps from the musicians, the house was nearly full. The four tiers sent forth a sparkle of diamonds, of silk, and of white arms and shoulders which rivalled the glitter of the vast crystal chandelier. The wide floor of serried stalls (those stalls of which one pair at least had gone for six pound ten) added their more sombre brilliance to the show, while far above, stretching away indefinitely to the very furthest roof, was the gallery (where but for Sullivan I should have been), a mass of black spotted with white faces.

Excitement was in the air: the expectation of seeing once again Rosetta Rosa, the girl with the golden throat, the mere girl who, two years ago, had in one brief month captured London, and who now, after a period of petulance, had decided to recapture London. On ordinary nights, for the inhabitants of boxes, the Opera is a social observance, an exhibition of jewels, something between an F.O. reception and a conversazione with music in the distance. But to-night the habitués confessed a genuine interest in the stage itself, abandoning their rôle of players. Dozens of times since then have I been to the Opera, and never have I witnessed the candid enthusiasm of that night. If London can be naïve, it was naïve then.

The conductor raised his baton. The orchestra ceased its tuning. The lights were lowered. Silence and stillness enwrapped the auditorium. And the quivering violins sighed out the first chords of the *Lohengrin* overture. For me, then, there existed nothing save the voluptuous music, to which I abandoned myself as to the fascination of a dream. But not for long. Just as the curtain rose, the door behind me gave a click, and Sullivan entered in all his magnificence. I jumped up. On his arm in the semi-darkness I discerned a tall, olive-pale woman, with large handsome features of Jewish cast, and large, liquid black eyes. She wore a dead-white gown, and over this a gorgeous cloak of purple and mauve.

"Emmeline, this is Carl," Sullivan whispered.

She smiled faintly, giving me her finger-tips, and then she suddenly took a step forward as if the better to examine my face. Her strange eyes met mine. She gave a little indefinable unnecessary "Ah!" and sank down into a chair, loosing my hand swiftly. I was going to say that she loosed my hand as if it had been the tail of a snake that she had picked up in mistake for something else. But that would leave the impression that her gesture was melodramatic, which it was not. Only there was in her demeanor a touch of the bizarre, ever so slight; yes, so slight that I could not be sure that I had not imagined it.

"The wife's a bit overwrought," Sullivan murmured in my ear. "Nerves, you know. Women are like that. Wait till you're married. Take no notice. She'll be all right soon."

I nodded and sat down. In a moment the music had resumed its sway over me.

I shall never forget my first sight of Rosetta Rosa as, robed with the modesty which the character of Elsa demands, she appeared on the stage to answer the accusation of Ortrud. For some moments she hesitated in the background, and then timidly, yet with what grandeur of mien, advanced towards the king. I knew then, as I know now, that hers was a loveliness of that imperious, absolute, dazzling kind which banishes from the hearts of men all moral conceptions, all considerations of right and wrong, and leaves therein nothing but worship and desire. Her acting, as she replied by gesture to the question of the king, was perfect in its realization of the simplicity of Elsa. Nevertheless I, at any rate, as I searched her features through the lorgnon that Mrs Sullivan had silently handed to me, could descry beneath the actress the girl—the spoilt and splendid child of Good Fortune, who in the very spring of youth had tasted the joy of sovereign power, that unique and terrible dominion over mankind which belongs to beauty alone.

Such a face as hers once seen is engraved eternally on the memory of its generation. And yet when, in a mood of lyrical and rapt ecstasy, she began her opening song, 'In Lichter Waffen Scheine,' her face was upon the instant forgotten. She became a Voice—pure, miraculous, all-compelling; and the listeners seemed to hold breath while the matchless melody wove round them its persuasive spell.

* * * * *

The first act was over, and Rosetta Rosa stood at the footlights bowing before the rolling and thunderous storms of applause, her hand in the hand of Alresca, the Lohengrin. That I have not till this moment mentioned Alresca, and that I mention him now merely as the man who happened to hold Rosa's hand, shows with what absolute sovereignty Rosa had dominated the scene. For as Rosa was among sopranos, so was Alresca among tenors—the undisputed star. Without other aid Alresca could fill the opera-house; did he not receive two hundred and fifty pounds a night? To put him in the same cast as Rosa was one of Cyril Smart's lavish freaks of expense.

As these two stood together Rosetta Rosa smiled at him; he gave her a timid glance and looked away.

When the clapping had ceased and the curtain hid the passions of the stage, I turned with a sigh of exhaustion and of pleasure to my hostess, and I was rather surprised to find that she showed not a trace of the nervous excitement which had marked her entrance into the box. She sat there, an excellent imitation of a woman of fashion, languid, unmoved, apparently a little bored, but finely conscious of doing the right thing.

"It's a treat to see anyone enjoy anything as you enjoy this music," she said to me. She spoke well, perhaps rather too carefully, and with a hint of the cockney accent.

"It runs in the family, you know, Mrs Smith," I replied, blushing for the ingenuousness which had pleased her.

"Don't call me Mrs Smith; call me Emmeline, as we are cousins. I shouldn't at all like it if I mightn't call you Carl. Carl is such a handsome name, and it suits you. Now, doesn't it, Sully?"

"Yes, darling," Sullivan answered nonchalantly. He was at the back of the box, and clearly it was his benevolent desire to give me fair opportunity of a *tête-à-tête* with his dark and languorous lady. Unfortunately, I was quite unpractised in the art of maintaining a *tête-à-tête* with dark and languorous ladies. Presently he rose.

"I must look up Smart," he said, and left us.

"Sullivan has been telling me about you. What a strange meeting! And so you are a doctor! You don't know how young you look. Why, I am old enough to be your mother!"

"Oh, no, you aren't," I said. At any rate, I knew enough to say that.

And she smiled.

"Personally," she went on, "I hate music—loathe it. But it's Sullivan's trade, and, of course, one must come here."

She waved a jewelled arm towards the splendid animation of the auditorium.

"But surely, Emmeline," I cried protestingly, "you didn't 'loathe' that first act. I never heard anything like it. Rosa was simply—well, I can't describe it."

She gazed at me, and a cloud of melancholy seemed to come into her eyes. And after a pause she said, in the strangest tone, very quietly:

"You're in love with her already."

And her eyes continued to hold mine.

"Who could help it?" I laughed.

She leaned towards me, and her left hand hung over the edge of the box.

"Women like Rosetta Rosa ought to be killed!" she said, with astonishing ferocity. Her rich, heavy contralto vibrated through me. She was excited again, that was evident. The nervous mood had overtaken her. The long pendent lobes of her ears crimsoned, and her opulent bosom heaved. I was startled. I was rather more than startled—I was frightened. I said to myself, "What a peculiar creature!"

"Why?" I questioned faintly.

"Because they are too young, too lovely, too dangerous," she responded with fierce emphasis. "And as for Rosa in particular—as for Rosa in particular—if you knew what I knew, what I've seen—"

"What have you seen?" I was bewildered. I began to wish that Sullivan had not abandoned me to her.

"Perhaps I'm wrong," she laughed.

She laughed, and sat up straight again, and resumed her excellent imitation of the woman of fashion, while I tried to behave as though I had found nothing singular in her behaviour.

"You know about our reception?" she asked vivaciously in another moment, playing with her fan.

"I'm afraid I don't."

"Where *have* you been, Carl?"

"I've been in Edinburgh," I said, "for my final."

"Oh!" she said. "Well, it's been paragraphed in all the papers. Sullivan is giving a reception in the Gold Rooms of the Grand Babylon Hotel. Of course, it will be largely theatrical,—Sullivan has to mix a good deal with that class, you know; it's his business,—but there will be a lot of good people there. You'll come, won't you? It's to celebrate the five hundredth performance of *My Queen*. Rosetta Rosa is coming."

"I shall be charmed. But I should have thought you wouldn't ask Rosa after what you've just said."

"Not ask Rosa! My dear Carl, she simply won't go *any*where. I know for a fact she declined Lady Casterby's invitation to meet a Serene Highness. Sir Cyril got her for me. She'll be the star of the show."

The theatre darkened once more. There were the usual preliminaries, and the orchestra burst into the prelude of the second act.

"Have you ever done any crystal-gazing?" Emmeline whispered.

And someone on the floor of the house hissed for silence.

I shook my head.

"You must try." Her voice indicated that she was becoming excited again. "At my reception there will be a spiritualism room. I'm a believer, you know."

I nodded politely, leaning over the front of the box to watch the conductor.

Then she set herself to endure the music.

Immediately the second act was over, Sullivan returned, bringing with him a short, slight, bald-headed man of about fifty. The two were just finishing a conversation on some stage matter.

"Smart, let me introduce to you my cousin, Carl Foster. Carl, this is Sir Cyril Smart."

My first feeling was one of surprise that a man so celebrated should be so insignificant to the sight. Yet as he looked at me I could somehow feel that here was an intelligence somewhat out of the common. At first he said little, and that little was said chiefly to my cousin's wife, but there was a quietude and firmness in his speech which had their own effect.

Sir Cyril had small eyes, and small features generally, including rather a narrow forehead. His nostrils, however, were well curved, and his thin, straight lips and square chin showed the stiffest determination. He looked fatigued, weary, and harassed; yet it did not appear that he complained of his lot; rather accepted it with sardonic humor. The cares of an opera season and of three other simultaneous managements weighed on him ponderously, but he supported the burden with stoicism.

"What is the matter with Alresca to-night?" Sullivan asked. "Suffering the pangs of jealousy, I suppose."

"Alresca," Sir Cyril replied, "is the greatest tenor living, and to-night he sings like a variety comedian. But it is not jealousy. There is one thing about Alresca that makes me sometimes think he is not an artist at all—he is incapable of being jealous. I have known hundreds of singers, and he is the one solitary bird among them of that plumage. No, it is not jealousy."

"Then what is it?"

"I wish I knew. He asked me to go and dine with him this afternoon. You know he dines at four o'clock. Of course, I went. What do you think he wanted me to do? He actually suggested that I should change the bill to-night! That showed me that something really was the matter, because he's the most modest and courteous man I have ever known, and he has a horror of disappointing the public. I asked him if he was hoarse. No. I asked him if he felt ill. No. But he was extremely depressed.

"'I'm quite well,' he said, 'and yet—' Then he stopped. 'And yet what?' It seemed as if I couldn't drag it out of him. Then all of a sudden he told me. 'My dear Smart,' he said, 'there is a misfortune coming to me. I feel it.' That's just what he said—'There's a misfortune coming to me. I feel it.' He's superstitious. They all are. Naturally, I set to work to soothe him. I did what I could. I talked about his liver in the usual way. But it had less than the usual effect. However, I persuaded him not to force me to change the bill."

Mrs Sullivan struck into the conversation.

"He isn't in love with Rosa, is he?" she demanded brusquely.

"In love with Rosa? Of course he isn't, my pet!" said Sullivan.

The wife glared at her husband as if angry, and Sullivan made a comic gesture of despair with his hands.

"Is he?" Mrs Sullivan persisted, waiting for Smart's reply.

"I never thought of that," said Sir Cyril simply. "No; I should say not, decidedly not … He may be, after all. I don't know. But if he were, that oughtn't to depress him. Even Rosa ought to be flattered by the admiration of a man like Alresca. Besides, so far as I know, they've seen very little of each other. They're too expensive to sing together often. There's only myself and Conried of New York who would dream of putting them in the same bill. I should say they hadn't sung together more than two or three times since the death of Lord Clarenceux; so, even if he has been making love to her, she's scarcely had time to refuse him—eh?"

"If he has been making love to Rosa," said Mrs Sullivan slowly, "whether she has refused him or not, it's a misfortune for him, that's all."

"Oh, you women! you women!" Sullivan smiled. "How fond you are of each other."

Mrs Sullivan disdained to reply to her spouse.

"And, let me tell you," she added, "he *has* been making love to her."

The talk momentarily ceased, and in order to demonstrate that I was not tongue-tied in the company of these celebrities, I ventured to inquire what Lord Clarenceux, whose riches and eccentricities had reached even the Scottish newspapers, had to do with the matter.

"Lord Clarenceux was secretly engaged to Rosa in Vienna," Sir Cyril replied. "That was about two and a half years ago. He died shortly afterwards. It was a terrible shock for her. Indeed, I have always thought that the shock had something to do with her notorious quarrel with us. She isn't naturally quarrelsome, so far as I can judge, though really I have seen very little of her."

"By the way, what was the real history of that quarrel?" said Sullivan. "I only know the beginning of it, and I expect Carl doesn't know even that, do you, Carl?"

"No," I murmured modestly. "But perhaps it's a State secret."

"Not in the least," Sir Cyril said, turning to me. "I first heard Rosa in Genoa—the opera-house there is more of a barn even than this, and a worse stage than this used to be, if that's possible. She was nineteen. Of course, I knew instantly that I had met with the chance of my life. In my time I have discovered eleven stars, but this was a sun. I engaged her at once, and she appeared here in the following July. She sang twelve times, and—well, you know the sensation there was. I had offered her twenty pounds a night in Genoa, and she seemed mighty enchanted.

"After her season here I offered her two hundred pounds a night for the following year; but Lord Clarenceux had met her then, and she merely said she would think it over. She wouldn't sign a contract. I was annoyed. My motto is, 'Never be annoyed,' but I was. Next to herself, she owed everything to me. She went to Vienna to fulfil an engagement, and Lord Clarenceux after her. I followed. I saw her, and I laid myself out to arrange terms of peace.

"I have had difficulties with *prime donne* before, scores of times. Yes; I have had experience." He laughed sardonically. "I thought I knew what to do. Generally a *prima donna* has either a pet dog or a pet parrot—sopranos go in for dogs, contraltos seem to prefer parrots. I have made a study of these agreeable animals, and I have found that through them their mistresses can be approached when all other avenues are closed. I can talk doggily to poodles in five languages, and in the art of administering sugar to the bird I am, I venture to think, unrivalled. But Rosa had no pets. And after a week's negotiation, I was compelled to own myself beaten. It was a disadvantage to me that she wouldn't lose her temper. She was too polite; she really was grateful for what I had done for her. She gave me no chance to work on her feelings. But beyond all this there was something strange about Rosa, something I have never been able to fathom. She isn't a child like most of 'em. She's as strong-headed as I am myself, every bit!"

He paused, as if inwardly working at the problem.

"Well, and how did you make it up?" Sullivan asked briskly.

(As for me, I felt as if I had come suddenly into the centre of the great world.)

"Oh, nothing happened for a time. She sang in Paris and America, and took her proper place as the first soprano in the world. I did without her, and managed very well. Then early this spring she sent her agent to see me, and offered to sing ten times for three thousand pounds. They can't keep away from London, you know. New York and Chicago are all very well for money, but if they don't sing in London people ask 'em why. I wanted to jump at the offer, but I pretended not to be eager. Up till then she had confined herself to French operas; so I said that London wouldn't stand an exclusively French repertoire from anyone, and would she sing in *Lohengrin*. She would. I suggested that she should open with *Lohengrin*, and she agreed. The price was stiffish, but I didn't quarrel with that. I never drive bargains. She is twenty-two now, or twenty-three; in a few more years she will want five hundred pounds a night, and I shall have to pay it."

"And how did she meet you?"

"With just the same cold politeness. And I understand her less than ever."

"She isn't English, I suppose?" I put in.

"English!" Sir Cyril ejaculated. "No one ever heard of a great English soprano. Unless you count Australia as England, and Australia wouldn't like that. No. That is another of her mysteries. No one knows where she emerged from. She speaks English and French with absolute perfection. Her Italian accent is beautiful. She talks German freely, but badly. I have heard that she speaks perfect Flemish,—which is curious,—but I do not know."

"Well," said Sullivan, nodding his head, "give me the theatrical as opposed to the operatic star. The theatrical star's bad enough, and mysterious enough, and awkward enough. But, thank goodness, she isn't polite—at least, those at the Diana aren't. You can speak your mind to 'em. And that reminds me, Smart, about that costume of Effie's in the first act of *My Queen*. Of course you'll insist—"

"Don't talk your horrid shop now, Sullivan," his wife said; and Sullivan didn't.

The prelude to the third act was played, and the curtain went up on the bridal chamber of Elsa and Lohengrin. Sir Cyril Smart rose as if to go, but lingered, eying the stage as a general might eye a battle-field from a neighbouring hill. The music of the two processions was heard approaching from the distance. Then, to the too familiar strains of the wedding march, the ladies began to enter on the right, and the gentlemen on the left. Elsa appeared amid her ladies, but there was no Lohengrin in the other crowd. The double chorus proceeded, and then a certain excitement was visible on the stage, and the conductor made signs with his left hand.

"Smart, what's wrong? Where's Alresca?" It was Sullivan who spoke.

"He'll sail in all right," Sir Cyril said calmly. "Don't worry."

The renowned impresario had advanced nearer to the front of our box, and was standing immediately behind my chair. My heart was beating violently with apprehension under my shirt-front. Where was Alresca? It was surely impossible that he should fail to appear! But he ought to have been on the stage, and he was not on the stage. I stole a glance at Sir Cyril's face. It was Napoleonic in its impassivity.

And I said to myself:

"He is used to this kind of thing. Naturally slips must happen sometimes."

Still, I could not control my excitement.

Emmeline's hand was convulsively clutching at the velvet-covered balustrade of the box.

"It'll be all right," I repeated to myself.

But when the moment came for the king to bless the bridal pair, and there was no Lohengrin to bless, even the impassive Sir Cyril seemed likely to be disturbed, and you could hear murmurs of apprehension from all parts of the house. The conductor, however, went doggedly on, evidently hoping for the best.

At last the end of the procession was leaving the stage, and Elsa was sitting on the bed alone. Still no Lohengrin. The violins arrived at the muted chord of B flat, which is Lohengrin's cue. They hung on it for a second, and then the conductor dropped his baton. A bell rang. The curtain descended. The lights were turned up, and there was a swift loosing of tongues in the house. People were pointing to Sir Cyril in our box. As for him, he seemed to be the only unmoved person in the audience.

"That's never occurred before in my time," he said. "Alresca was not mistaken. Something has happened. I must go."

But he did not go. And I perceived that, though the calm of his demeanor was unimpaired, this unprecedented calamity had completely robbed him of his power of initiative. He could not move. He was nonplussed.

The door of the box opened, and an official with a blazing diamond in his shirt-front entered hurriedly.

"What is it, Nolan?"

"There's been an accident to Monsieur Alresca, Sir Cyril, and they want a doctor."

It was the chance of a lifetime! I ought to have sprung up and proudly announced, "I'm a doctor." But did I? No! I was so timid, I was so unaccustomed to being a doctor, that I dared not for the life of me utter a word. It was as if I was almost ashamed of being a doctor. I wonder if my state of mind will be understood.

"Carl's a doctor," said Sullivan.

How I blushed!

"Are you?" said Sir Cyril, suddenly emerging from his condition of suspended activity. "I never guessed it. Come along with us, will you?"

"With pleasure," I answered as briskly as I could.

III

THE CRY OF ALRESCA

A S I LEFT THE BOX in the wake of Sir Cyril and Mr Nolan, Sullivan jumped up to follow us, and the last words I heard were from Emmeline.

"Sullivan, stay here. You shall not go near that woman," she exclaimed in feverish and appealing tones: excitement had once more overtaken her. And Sullivan stayed.

"Berger here?" Sir Cyril asked hurriedly of Nolan.

"Yes, sir."

"Send someone for him. I'll get him to take Alresca's part. He'll have to sing it in French, but that won't matter. We'll make a new start at the duet."

"But Rosa?" said Nolan.

"Rosa! *She's* not hurt, is she?"

"No, sir. But she's upset."

"What the devil is she upset about?"

"The accident. She's practically useless. We shall never persuade her to sing again to-night."

"Oh, damn!" Sir Cyril exclaimed. And then quite quietly: "Well, run and tell 'em, then. Shove yourself in front of the curtain, my lad, and make a speech. Say it's nothing serious, but just sufficient to stop the performance. Apologize, grovel, flatter 'em, appeal to their generosity—you know."

"Yes, Sir Cyril."

And Nolan disappeared on his mission of appeasing the audience.

We had traversed the flagged corridor. Sir Cyril opened a narrow door at the end.

"Follow me," he called out. "This passage is quite dark, but quite straight."

It was not a passage; it was a tunnel. I followed the sound of his footsteps, my hands outstretched to feel a wall on either side. It seemed a long way, but suddenly we stepped into twilight. There was a flight of steps which we descended, and at the foot of the steps a mutilated commissionaire, ornamented with medals, on guard.

"Where is Monsieur Alresca?" Sir Cyril demanded.

"Behind the back-cloth, where he fell, sir," answered the commissionaire, saluting.

I hurried after Sir Cyril, and found myself amid a most extraordinary scene of noise and confusion on the immense stage. The entire personnel of the house seemed to be present: a crowd apparently consisting of thousands of people, and which really did comprise some hundreds. Never before had I had such a clear conception of the elaborate human machinery necessary to the production of even a comparatively simple lyric work like *Lohengrin*. Richly clad pages and maids-of-honour, all white and gold and rouge, mingled with shirt-sleeved carpenters and scene-shifters in a hysterical rabble; chorus-masters, footmen in livery, loungers in evening dress, girls in picture hats, members of the orchestra with instruments under their arms, and even children, added variety to the throng. And, round about, gigantic "flats" of wood and painted canvas rose to the flies, where their summits were lost in a maze of ropes and pulleys. Beams of light, making visible great clouds of dust, shot forth from hidden sources. Voices came down from the roof, and from far below ascended the steady pulsation of a dynamo. I was bewildered.

Sir Cyril pushed ahead, without saying a word, without even remonstrating when his minions omitted to make way for him. Right at the back of the stage, and almost in the centre, the crowd was much thicker. And at last, having penetrated it, we came upon a sight which I am not likely to forget. Rosa, in all the splendor of the bridal costume, had passed her arms under Alresca's armpits, and so raised his head and shoulders against her breast. She was gazing into the face of the spangled knight, and the tears were falling from her eyes into his.

"My poor Alresca! My poor Alresca!" she kept murmuring.

Pressing on these two were a distinguished group consisting of the King, the Herald, Ortrud, Telramund, and several more. And Ortrud was cautiously feeling Alresca's limbs with her jewel-laden fingers. I saw instantly that Alresca was unconscious.

"Please put him down, mademoiselle."

These were the first words that I ever spoke to Rosetta Rosa, and, out of sheer acute nervousness, I uttered them roughly, in a tone of surly command. I was astonished at myself. I was astonished at my own voice. She glanced up at me and hesitated. No doubt she was unaccustomed to such curt orders.

"Please put him down at once," I repeated, trying to assume a bland, calm, professional, authoritative manner, and not in the least succeeding. "It is highly dangerous to lift an unconscious person from a recumbent position."

Why I should have talked like an article in a medical dictionary instead of like a human being I cannot imagine.

"This is a doctor—Mr Carl Foster," Sir Cyril explained smoothly, and she laid Alresca's head gently on the bare planks of the floor.

"Will everyone kindly stand aside, and I will examine him."

No one moved. The King continued his kingly examination of the prone form. Not a fold of Ortrud's magnificent black robe was disturbed. Then Sir Cyril translated my request into French and into German, and these legendary figures of the Middle Ages withdrew a little, fixing themselves with difficulty into the common multitude that pressed on them from without. I made them retreat still further. Rosetta Rosa moved gravely to one side.

Almost immediately Alresca opened his eyes, and murmured faintly, "My thigh."

I knelt down, but not before Rosa had sprung forward at the sound of his voice, and kneeling close by my side had clasped his hand. I tried to order her away, but my tongue could not form the words. I could only look at her mutely, and there must have been an effective appeal in my eyes, for she got up, nodding an acquiescence, and stood silent and tense a yard from Alresca's feet. With a violent effort I nerved myself to perform my work. The voice of Nolan, speaking to the audience, and then a few sympathetic cheers, came vaguely from the other side of the big curtain, and then the orchestra began to play the National Anthem.

The left thigh was broken near the knee-joint. So much I ascertained at once. As I manipulated the limb to catch the sound of the crepitus the injured man screamed, and he was continually in very severe pain. He did not, however, again lose consciousness.

"I must have a stretcher, and he must be carried to a room. I can't do anything here," I said to Sir Cyril. "And you had better send for a first-rate surgeon. Sir Francis Shorter would do very well—102 Manchester Square, I think the address is. Tell him it's a broken thigh. It will be a serious case."

"Let me send for my doctor—Professor Eugene Churt," Rosa said. "No one could be more skilful."

"Pardon me," I protested, "Professor Churt is a physician of great authority, but he is not a surgeon, and here he would be useless."

She bowed—humbly, as I thought.

With such materials as came to hand I bound Alresca's legs together, making as usual the sound leg fulfil the function of a splint to the other one, and he was placed on a stretcher. It was my first case, and it is impossible for me to describe my shyness and awkwardness as the men who were to carry the stretcher to the dressing-room looked silently to me for instructions.

"Now," I said, "take short steps, keep your knees bent, but don't on any account keep step. As gently as you can—all together—lift."

Rosa followed the little procession as it slowly passed through the chaotic anarchy of the stage. Alresca was groaning, his eyes closed. Suddenly he opened them, and it seemed as though he caught sight of her for the first time. He lifted his head, and the sweat stood in drops on his brow.

"Send her away!" he cried sharply, in an agony which was as much mental as physical. "She is fatal to me."

The bearers stopped in alarm at this startling outburst; but I ordered them forward, and turned to Rosa. She had covered her face with her hands, and was sobbing.

"Please go away," I said. "It is very important he should not be agitated."

Without quite intending to do so, I touched her on the shoulder.

"Alresca doesn't mean that!" she stammered.

Her blue eyes were fixed on me, luminous through her tears, and I feasted on all the lovely curves of that incomparable oval which was her face.

"I am sure he doesn't," I answered. "But you had better go, hadn't you?"

"Yes," she said, "I will go."

"Forgive my urgency," I murmured. Then she drew back and vanished in the throng.

In the calm of the untidy dressing-room, with the aid of Alresca's valet, I made my patient as comfortable as possible on a couch. And then I had one of the many surprises of my life. The door opened, and old Toddy entered. No inhabitant of the city of Edinburgh would need explanations on the subject of Toddy MacWhirter. The first surgeon of Scotland, his figure is familiar from one end of the town to the other—and even as far as Leith and Portobello. I trembled. And my reason for trembling was that the celebrated bald expert had quite recently examined me for my Final in surgery. On that dread occasion I had made one bad blunder, so ridiculous that Toddy's mood had passed suddenly from grim ferociousness to wild northern hilarity. I think I am among the few persons in the world who have seen and heard Toddy MacWhirter laugh.

I hoped that he would not remember me, but, like many great men, he had a disconcertingly good memory for faces.

"Ah!" he said, "I've seen ye before."

"You have, sir."

"You are the callant who told me that the medulla oblongata—"

"Please—" I entreated.

Perhaps he would not have let me off had not Sir Cyril stood immediately behind him. The impresario explained that Toddy MacWhirter (the impresario did not so describe him) had been in the audience, and had offered his services.

"What is it?" asked Toddy, approaching Alresca.

"Fracture of the femur."

"Simple, of course."

"Yes, sir, but so far as I can judge, of a somewhat peculiar nature. I've sent round to King's College Hospital for splints and bandages."

Toddy took off his coat.

"We shan't need ye, Sir Cyril," said he casually.

And Sir Cyril departed.

In an hour the limb was set—a masterly display of skill—and, except to give orders, Toddy had scarcely spoken another word. As he was washing his hands in a corner of the dressing-room he beckoned to me.

"How was it caused?" he whispered.

"No one seems to know, sir."

"Doesn't matter much, anyway! Let him lie a wee bit, and then get him home. Ye'll have no trouble with him, but there'll be no more warbling and cutting capers for him this yet awhile."

And Toddy, too, went. He had showed not the least curiosity as to Alresca's personality, and I very much doubt whether he had taken the trouble to differentiate between the finest tenor in Europe and a chorus-singer. For Toddy, Alresca was simply an individual who sang and cut capers.

I made the necessary dispositions for the transport of Alresca in an hour's time to his flat in the Devonshire Mansion, and then I sat down near him. He was white and weak, but perfectly conscious. He had proved himself to be an admirable patient. Even in the very crisis of the setting his personal distinction and his remarkable and finished politeness had suffered no eclipse. And now he lay there, with his silky moustache disarranged and his hair damp, exactly as I had once seen him on the couch in the garden by the sea in the third act of *Tristan*, the picture of nobility. He could not move, for the sufficient reason that a strong splint ran from his armpit to his ankle, but his arms were free, and he raised his left hand, and beckoned me with an irresistible gesture to come quite close to him.

I smiled encouragingly and obeyed.

"My kind friend," he murmured, "I know not your name."

His English was not the English of an Englishman, but it was beautiful in its exotic quaintness.

"My name is Carl Foster," I said. "It will be better for you not to talk."

He made another gesture of protest with that wonderful left hand of his.

"Monsieur Foster, I must talk to Mademoiselle Rosa."

"Impossible," I replied. "It really is essential that you should keep quiet."

"Kind friend, grant me this wish. When I have seen her I shall be better. It will do me much good."

There was such a desire in his eyes, such a persuasive plaintiveness in his voice, that, against my judgment, I yielded.

"Very well," I said. "But I am afraid I can only let you see her for five minutes."

The hand waved compliance, and I told the valet to go and inquire for Rosa.

"She is here, sir," said the valet on opening the door. I jumped up. There she was, standing on the door-mat in the narrow passage! Yet I had been out of the room twice, once to speak to Sir Cyril Smart, and once to answer an inquiry from my cousin Sullivan, and I had not seen her.

She was still in the bridal costume of Elsa, and she seemed to be waiting for permission to enter. I went outside to her, closing the door.

"Sir Cyril would not let me come," she said. "But I have escaped him. I was just wondering if I dared peep in. How is he?"

"He is getting on splendidly," I answered. "And he wants to have a little chat with you."

"And may he?"

"If you will promise to be very, very ordinary, and not to excite him."

"I promise," she said with earnestness.

"Remember," I added, "quite a little, tiny chat!"

She nodded and went in, I following. Upon catching sight of her, Alresca's face broke into an exquisite, sad smile. Then he gave his valet a glance, and the valet crept from the room. I, as in professional duty bound, remained. The most I could do was to retire as far from the couch, and pretend to busy myself with the rolling up of spare bandages.

"My poor Rosa," I heard Alresca begin.

The girl had dropped to her knees by his side, and taken his hand.

"How did it happen, Alresca? Tell me."

"I cannot tell you! I saw—saw something, and I fell, and caught my leg against some timber, and I don't remember any more."

"Saw something? What did you see?"

There was a silence.

"Were you frightened?" Rosa continued softly.

Then another silence.

"Yes," said Alresca at length, "I was frightened."

"What was it?"

"I say I cannot tell you. I do not know."

"You are keeping something from me, Alresca," she exclaimed passionately.

I was on the point of interfering in order to bring the colloquy to an end, but I hesitated. They appeared to have forgotten that I was there.

"How so?" said Alresca in a curious whisper. "I have nothing to keep from you, my dear child."

"Yes," she said, "you are keeping something from me. This afternoon you told Sir Cyril that you were expecting a misfortune. Well, the misfortune has occurred to you. How did you guess that it was coming? Then, to-night, as they were carrying you away on that stretcher, do you remember what you said?"

"What did I say?"

"You remember, don't you?" Rosa faltered.

"I remember," he admitted. "But that was nonsense. I didn't know what I was saying. My poor Rosa, I was delirious. And that is just why I wished to see you—in order to explain to you that that was nonsense. You must forget what I said. Remember only that I love you."

("So Emmeline was right," I reflected.)

Abruptly Rosa stood up.

"You must not love me, Alresca," she said in a shaking voice. "You ask me to forget something; I will try. You, too, must forget something—your love."

"But last night," he cried, in accents of an almost intolerable pathos—"last night, when I hinted—you did not—did not speak like this, Rosetta."

I rose. I had surely no alternative but to separate them. If I allowed the interview to be prolonged the consequences to my patient might be extremely serious. Yet again I hesitated. It was the sound of Rosa's sobbing that arrested me.

Once more she dropped to her knees.

"Alresca!" she moaned.

He seized her hand and kissed it.

And then I came forward, summoning all my courage to assert the doctor's authority. And in the same instant Alresca's features, which had been the image of intense joy, wholly changed their expression, and were transformed into the embodiment of fear. With a look of frightful terror he pointed with one white hand to the blank wall opposite. He tried to sit up, but the splint prevented him. Then his head fell back.

"It is there!" he moaned. "Fatal! My Rosa—"

The words died in his mouth, and he swooned.

As for Rosetta Rosa, I led her from the room.

IV

ROSA'S SUMMONS

Everyone knows the Gold Rooms at the Grand Babylon on the Embankment. They are immense, splendid, and gorgeous; they possess more gold leaf to the square inch than any music-hall in London. They were designed to throw the best possible light on humanity in the mass, to illuminate effectively not only the shoulders of women, but also the sombreness of men's attire. Not a tint on their walls that has not been profoundly studied and mixed and laid with a view to the great aim. Wherefore, when the electric clusters glow in the ceiling, and the "after-dinner" band (that unique corporation of British citizens disguised as wild Hungarians) breathes and pants out its after-dinner melodies from the raised platform in the main salon, people regard this *coup d'oeil* with awe, and feel glad that they are in the dazzling picture, and even the failures who are there imagine that they have succeeded. Wherefore, also, the Gold Rooms of the Grand Babylon are expensive, and only philanthropic societies, plutocrats, and the Titans of the theatrical world may persuade themselves that they can afford to engage them.

It was very late when I arrived at my cousin Sullivan's much advertised reception. I had wished not to go at all, simply because I was inexperienced and nervous; but both he and his wife were so good-natured and so obviously anxious to be friendly, that I felt bound to appear, if only for a short time. As I stood in the first room, looking vaguely about me at the lively throng of resplendent actresses who chattered and smiled so industriously and with such abundance of gesture to the male acquaintances who surrounded them, I said to myself that I was singularly out of place there.

I didn't know a soul, and the stream of arrivals having ceased, neither Sullivan nor Emmeline was immediately visible. The moving picture was at once attractive and repellent to me. It became instantly apparent that the majority of the men and women there had but a single interest in life, that of centring attention upon themselves; and their various methods of reaching this desirable end were curious and wonderful in the extreme. For all practical purposes, they were still on the boards which they had left but an hour or two before. It seemed as if they regarded the very orchestra in the light of a specially contrived accompaniment to their several actions and movements. As they glanced carelessly at me, I felt that they held me as a foreigner, as one outside that incredible little world of theirs which they call 'the profession.' And so I felt crushed, with a faint resemblance to a worm. You see, I was young.

I walked through towards the main salon, and in the doorway between the two rooms I met a girl of striking appearance, who was followed by two others. I knew her face well, having seen it often in photograph shops; it was the face of Marie Deschamps, the popular divette of the Diana Theatre, the leading lady of Sullivan's long-lived musical comedy, *My Queen*. I needed no second glance to convince me that Miss Deschamps was a very important personage indeed, and, further, that a large proportion of her salary of seventy-five pounds a week was expended in the suits and trappings of triumph. If her dress did not prove that she was on the topmost bough of the tree, then nothing could. Though that night is still recent history, times have changed. Divettes could do more with three hundred a month then than they can with eight hundred now.

As we passed she examined me with a curiosity whose charm was its frankness. Of course, she put me out of countenance, particularly when she put her hand on my sleeve. Divettes have the right to do these things.

"I know who you are," she said, laughing and showing her teeth. "You are dear old Sully's cousin; he pointed you out to me the other night when you were at the Diana. Now, don't say you aren't, or I shall look such a fool; and for goodness' sake don't say you don't know me—because everyone knows me, and if they don't they ought to."

I was swept away by the exuberance of her attack, and, blushing violently, I took the small hand which she offered, and assured her that I was in fact Sullivan Smith's cousin, and her sincere admirer.

"That's all right," she said, raising her superb shoulders after a special manner of her own. "Now you shall take me to Sullivan, and he shall introduce us. Any friend of dear old Sully's is a friend of mine. How do you like my new song?"

"What new song?" I inquired incautiously.

"Why, 'Who milked the cow?' of course."

I endeavoured to give her to understand that it had made an indelible impression on me; and with such like converse we went in search of Sullivan, while everyone turned to observe the unknown shy young man who was escorting Marie Deschamps.

"Here he is," my companion said at length, as we neared the orchestra, "listening to the band. He should have a band, the little dear! Sullivan, introduce me to your cousin."

"Charmed—delighted." And Sullivan beamed with pleasure. "Ah, my young friend," he went on to me, "you know your way about fairly well. But there! medical students—they're all alike. Well, what do you think of the show?"

"Hasn't he done it awfully well, Mr Foster?" said Miss Deschamps.

I said that I should rather think he had.

"Look here," said Sullivan, becoming grave and dropping his voice, "there are four hundred invitations, and it'll cost me seven hundred and fifty pounds. But it pays. You know that, don't you, Marie? Look at the advertisement! And I've got a lot of newspaper chaps here. It'll be in every paper to-morrow. I reckon I've done this thing on the right lines. It's only a reception, of course, but let me tell you I've seen after the refreshments—not snacks—re*fresh*ments, mind you! And there's a smoke-room for the boys, and the wife's got a spiritualism-room, and there's the show in this room. Some jolly good people here, too—not all chorus girls and walking gents. Are they, Marie?"

"You bet not," the lady replied.

"Rosetta Rosa's coming, and she won't go quite everywhere—not quite! By the way, it's about time she *did* come." He looked at his watch.

"Ah, Mr Foster," the divette said, "you must tell me all about that business. I'm told you were there, and that there was a terrible scene."

"What business?" I inquired.

"At the Opera the other night, when Alresca broke his thigh. Didn't you go behind and save his life?"

"I didn't precisely save his life, but I attended to him."

"They say he is secretly married to Rosa. Is that so?"

"I really can't say, but I think not."

"What did she say to him when she went into his dressing-room? I know all about it, because one of our girls has a sister who's in the Opera chorus, and her sister saw Rosa go in. I do want to know what she said, and what he said."

An impulse seized me to invent a harmless little tale for the diversion of Marie Deschamps. I was astonished at my own enterprise. I perceived that I was getting accustomed to the society of greatness.

"Really?" she exclaimed, when I had finished.

"I assure you."

"He's teasing," Sullivan said.

"Mr Foster wouldn't do such a thing," she observed, drawing herself up, and I bowed.

A man with an eye-glass came and began to talk confidently in Sullivan's ear, and Sullivan had to leave us.

"See you later," he smiled. "Keep him out of mischief, Marie. And I say, Carl, the wife said I was to tell you particularly to go into her crystal-gazing room. Don't forget."

"I'll go, too," Miss Deschamps said. "You may take me there now, if you please. And then I must go down to where the champagne is flowing. But not with you, not with you, Mr Foster. There are other gentlemen here very anxious for the post. Now come along."

We made our way out of the stir and noise of the grand salon, Marie Deschamps leaning on my arm in the most friendly and confiding way in the world, and presently we found ourselves in a much smaller apartment crowded with whispering seekers after knowledge of the future. This room was dimly lighted from the ceiling by a single electric light, whose shade was a queer red Japanese lantern. At the other end of it were double curtains. These opened just as we entered, and Emmeline appeared, leading by the hand a man who was laughing nervously.

"Your fortune, ladies and gentlemen, your fortune!" she cried pleasantly. Then she recognized me, and her manner changed, or I fancied that it did.

"Ah, Carl, so you've arrived!" she exclaimed, coming forward and ignoring all her visitors except Marie and myself.

"Yes, Emmeline, dear," said Marie, "we've come. And, please, I want to see something in the crystal. How do you do it?"

Emmeline glanced around.

"Sullivan said my crystal-gazing would be a failure," she smiled. "But it isn't, is it? I came in here as soon as I had done receiving, and I've already had I don't know how many clients. I shan't be able to stop long, you know. The fact is, Sullivan doesn't like me being here at all. He thinks it not right of the hostess—"

"But it's perfectly charming of you!" someone put in.

"Perfectly delicious!" said Marie.

"Now, who shall I take first?" Emmeline asked, puzzled.

"Oh, me, of course!" Marie Deschamps replied without a hesitation or a doubt, though she and I had come in last. And the others acquiesced, because Marie was on the topmost bough of all.

"Come along, then," said Emmeline, relieved.

I made as if to follow them.

"No, Mr Foster," said Marie. "You just stay here, and don't listen."

The two women disappeared behind the portière, and a faint giggle, soon suppressed, came through the portière from Marie.

I obeyed her orders, but as I had not the advantage of knowing a single person in that outer room, I took myself off for a stroll, in the hope of encountering Rosetta Rosa. Yes, certainly in the hope of encountering Rosetta Rosa! But in none of the thronged chambers did I discover her.

When I came back, the waiting-room for prospective crystal-gazers was empty, and Emmeline herself was just leaving it.

"What!" I exclaimed. "All over?"

"Yes," she said; "Sullivan has sent for me. You see, of course, one has to mingle with one's guests. Only they're really Sullivan's guests."

"And what about me?" I said. "Am I not going to have a look into the crystal?"

I had, as a matter of fact, not the slightest interest in her crystal at that instant. I regarded the crystal as a harmless distraction of hers, and I was being simply jocular when I made that remark. Emmeline, however, took it seriously. As her face had changed when she first saw me in the box at the Opera, and again to-night when she met me and Marie Deschamps on my arm, so once more it changed now.

"Do you really want to?" she questioned me, in her thrilling voice.

My soul said: "It's all rubbish—but suppose there is something in it, after all?"

And I said aloud:

"Yes."

"Come, then."

We passed through the room with the red Japanese lantern, and lo! the next room was perfectly dark save for an oval of white light which fell slantingly on a black marble table. The effect was rather disconcerting at first; but the explanation was entirely simple. The light came from an electric table-lamp (with a black cardboard shade arranged at an angle) which stood on the table. As my eyes grew accustomed to the obscurity I discovered two chairs.

"Sit down," said Emmeline.

And she and I each took one of the chairs, at opposite sides of the table.

Emmeline was magnificently attired. As I looked at her in the dimness across the table, she drummed her fingers on the marble, and then she bent her face to glance within the shade of the lamp, and for a second her long and heavy, yet handsome, features were displayed to the minutest part in the blinding ray of the lamp, and the next second they were in obscurity again. It was uncanny. I was impressed; and all the superstition which, like a snake, lies hidden in the heart of every man, stirred vaguely and raised its head.

"Carl—" Emmeline began, and paused.

The woman indubitably did affect me strangely. Hers was a lonely soul, an unusual mixture of the absolutely conventional and of something quite else—something bizarre, disturbing, and inexplicable. I was conscious of a feeling of sympathy for her.

"Well?" I murmured.

"Do you believe in the supernatural?"

"I neither believe nor disbelieve," I replied, "for I have never met with anything that might be a manifestation of it. But I may say that I am not a hard and fast materialist." And I added: "Do *you* believe in it?"

"Of course," she snapped.

"Then, if you really believe, if it's so serious to you, why do you make a show of it for triflers?".

"Ah!" she breathed. "Some of them do make me angry. They like to play at having dealings with the supernatural. But I thought the crystal would be such a good thing for Sullivan's reception. It is very important to Sullivan that this should be a great success—our first large public reception, you know. Sullivan says we must advertise ourselves."

The explanation of her motives was given so naïvely, so simply and unaffectedly, that it was impossible to take exception to it.

"Where's the crystal?" I inquired.

"It is here," she said, and she rolled a glass ball with the suddenness that had the appearance of magic from the dark portion of the table's surface into the oval of light. And it was so exactly spherical, and the table top was so smooth that it would not stay where it was put, and she had to hold it there with her ringed hand.

"So that's it," I remarked.

"Carl," she said, "it is only right I should warn you. Some weeks ago I saw in the crystal the face of a man whom I did not know. I saw it again and again—and always the same scene. Then I saw you at the Opera last week, and Sullivan introduced you as his cousin that he talks about sometimes. Did you notice that night that I behaved rather queerly?"

"Yes." I spoke shortly.

"You are the man whom I saw in the crystal."

"Really?" I ejaculated, smiling, or at least trying to smile. "And what is the scene of which I am part?"

"You are standing—But no!"

She abruptly ceased speaking and coughed, clearing her throat, and she fixed her large eyes on me. Outside I could hear the distant strain of the orchestra, and the various noises of a great crowd of people. But this little dark room, with its sharply defined oval of light, was utterly shut off from the scene of gaiety. I was aware of an involuntary shiver, and for the life of me I could not keep my gaze steadily on the face of the tall woman who sat so still, with such impressiveness, on the other side of the table. I waited for her to proceed, and after what seemed a long interval she spoke again:

"You aren't afraid, are you?" she demanded.

"Of course I'm not."

"Then you shall look into the crystal and try to see what I saw. I will not tell you. You shall try to see for yourself. You may succeed, if I help you. Now, try to free your mind from every thought, and look earnestly. *Look*!"

I drew the globe towards me from under her fingers.

"Rum!" I murmured to myself.

Then I strenuously fixed my eyes on the glinting depths of the crystal, full of strange, shooting fires; but I could see nothing whatever.

"No go!" I said. "You'll have to tell me what you saw."

"Patience. There is time yet. Look again. Take my hand in your right hand."

I obeyed, and we sat together in the tense silence. After a few minutes, the crystal darkened and then slowly cleared. I trembled with an uneasy anticipation.

"You see something," she breathed sorrowfully in my ear.

"Not yet, not yet," I whispered. "But it is coming. Yes, I see myself, and—and—a woman—a very pretty woman. I am clasping her hand."

"Don't you recognize the woman?" Again Emmeline's voice vibrated like a lamentation in my ear. I did recognize the woman, and the sweat stood on my brow.

"It is Rosetta Rosa!"

"And what else do you see?" my questioner pursued remorselessly.

"I see a figure behind us," I stammered, "but what figure I cannot make out. It is threatening me. It is threatening me! It is a horrible thing. It will kill me! Ah—!"

I jumped up with a nervous movement. The crystal, left to itself, rolled off the table to the floor, and fell with a thud unbroken on the soft carpet. And I could hear the intake of Emmeline's breath.

At that moment the double portière was pulled apart, and someone stood there in the red light from the Japanese lantern.

"Is Mr Foster here? I want him to come with me," said a voice. And it was the voice of Rosa.

Just behind her was Sullivan.

"I expected you'd be here," laughed Sullivan.

V

THE DAGGER AND THE MAN

ROSETTA ROSA AND I THREADED through the crowd towards the Embankment entrance of the Gold Rooms. She had spoken for a few moments with Emmeline, who went pale with satisfaction at the candid friendliness of her tone, and she had chatted quite gaily with Sullivan himself; and we had all been tremendously impressed by her beauty and fine grace—I certainly not the least. And then she had asked me, with a quality of mysteriousness in her voice, to see her to her carriage.

And, with her arm in mine, it was impossible for me to believe that she could influence, in any evil way, my future career. That she might be the cause of danger to my life seemed ridiculous. She was the incarnation of kindliness and simplicity. She had nothing about her of the sinister, and further, with all her transcendent beauty and charm, she was also the incarnation of the matter-of-fact. I am obliged to say this, though I fear that it may impair for some people the vision of her loveliness and her unique personality. She was the incarnation of the matter-of-fact, because she appeared to be invariably quite unconscious of the supremacy of her talents. She was not weighed down by them, as many artists of distinction are weighed down. She carried them lightly, seemingly unaware that they existed. Thus no one could have guessed that that very night she had left the stage of the Opera after an extraordinary triumph in her greatest rôle—that of Isolde in *Tristan*.

And so her presence by my side soothed away almost at once the excitation and the spiritual disturbance of the scene through which I had just passed with Emmeline; and I was disposed, if not to laugh at the whole thing, at any rate to regard it calmly, dispassionately, as one of the various inexplicable matters with which one meets in a world absurdly called prosaic. I was sure that no trick had been played upon me. I was sure that I had actually seen in the crystal what I had described to Emmeline, and that she, too, had seen it. But then, I argued, such an experience might be the result of hypnotic suggestion, or of thought transference, or of some other imperfectly understood agency... Rosetta Rosa an instrument of misfortune! No!

When I looked at her I comprehended how men have stopped at nothing for the sake of love, and how a woman, if only she be beautiful enough, may wield a power compared to which the sway of a Tsar, even a Tsar unhampered by Dumas, is impotence itself. Even at that early stage I had begun to be a captive to her. But I did not believe that her rule was malign.

"Mr Foster," she said, "I have asked you to see me to my carriage, but really I want you to do more than that. I want you to go with me to poor Alresca's. He is progressing satisfactorily, so far as I can judge, but the dear fellow is thoroughly depressed. I saw him this afternoon, and he wished, if I met you here to-night, that I should bring you to him. He has a proposition to make to you, and I hope you will accept it."

"I shall accept it, then," I said.

She pulled out a tiny gold watch, glistening with diamonds.

"It is half-past one," she said. "We might be there in ten minutes. You don't mind it being late, I suppose. We singers, you know, have our own hours."

In the foyer we had to wait while the carriage was called. I stood silent, and perhaps abstracted, at her elbow, absorbed in the pride and happiness of being so close to her, and looking forward with a tremulous pleasure to the drive through London at her side. She was dressed in grey, with a large ermine-lined cloak, and she wore no ornaments except a thin jewelled dagger in her lovely hair.

All at once I saw that she flushed, and, following the direction of her eyes, I beheld Sir Cyril Smart, with a startled gaze fixed immovably on her face. Except the footmen and the attendants attached to the hotel, there were not half a dozen people in the entrance-hall at this moment. Sir Cyril was nearly as white as the marble floor. He made a step forward, and then stood still. She, too, moved towards him, as it seemed, involuntarily.

"Good evening, Miss Rosa," he said at length, with a stiff inclination. She responded, and once more they stared at each other. I wondered whether they had quarrelled again, or whether both were by some mischance simultaneously indisposed. Surely they must have already met during the evening at the Opera!

Then Rosa, with strange deliberation, put her hand to her hair and pulled out the jewelled dagger.

"Sir Cyril," she said, "you seem fascinated by this little weapon. Do you recognize it?"

He made no answer, nor moved, but I noticed that his hands were tightly clenched.

"You do recognize it, Sir Cyril?"

At last he nodded.

"Then take it. The dagger shall be yours. To-night, within the last minute, I think I have suddenly discovered that, next to myself, you have the best right to it."

He opened his lips to speak, but made no sound.

"See," she said. "It is a real dagger, sharp and pointed."

Throwing back her cloak with a quick gesture, she was about to prick the skin of her left arm between the top of her long glove and the sleeve of her low-cut dress. But Sir Cyril, and I also, jumped to stop her.

"Don't do that," I said. "You might hurt yourself."

She glanced at me, angry for the instant; but her anger dissolved in an icy smile.

"Take it, Sir Cyril, to please me."

Her intonation was decidedly peculiar.

And Sir Cyril took the dagger.

"Miss Rosa's carriage," a commissionaire shouted, and, beckoning to me, the girl moved imperiously down the steps to the courtyard. There was no longer a smile on her face, which had a musing and withdrawn expression. Sir Cyril stood stock-still, holding the dagger. What the surrounding lackeys thought of this singular episode I will not guess. Indeed, the longer I live, the less I care to meditate upon what lackeys *do* think. But that the adventures of their employers provide them with ample food for thought there can be no doubt.

Rosa's horses drew us swiftly away from the Grand Babylon Hotel, and it seemed that she wished to forget or to ignore the remarkable incident. For some moments she sat silent, her head slightly bent, her cloak still thrown back, but showing no sign of agitation beyond a slightly hurried heaving of the bosom.

I was discreet enough not to break in upon her reflections by any attempt at conversation, for it seemed to me that what I had just witnessed had been a sudden and terrible crisis, not only in the life of Sir Cyril, but also in that of the girl whose loveliness was dimly revealed to me in the obscurity of the vehicle.

We had got no further than Trafalgar Square when she aroused herself, looked at me, and gave a short laugh.

"I suppose," she remarked, "that a doctor can't cure every disease?"

"Scarcely," I replied.

"Not even a young doctor?" she said with comical gravity.

"Not even a young doctor," I gravely answered.

Then we both laughed.

"You must excuse my fun," she said. "I can't help it, especially when my mind is disturbed."

"Why do you ask me?" I inquired. "Was it just a general observation caused by the seriousness of my countenance, or were you thinking of something in particular?"

"I was thinking of Alresca," she murmured, "my poor Alresca. He is the rarest gentleman and the finest artist in Europe, and he is suffering."

"Well," I said, "one can't break one's thigh for nothing."

"It is not his thigh. It is something else."

"What?"

She shook her head, to indicate her inability to answer.

Here I must explain that, on the morning after the accident, I had taken a hansom to the Devonshire Mansion with the intention of paying a professional visit to Alresca. I was not altogether certain that I ought to regard the case as mine, but I went. Immediately before my hansom, however, there had drawn up another hansom in front of the portals of the Devonshire, and out of that other hansom had stepped the famous Toddy MacWhirter. Great man as Toddy was, he had an eye on 'saxpences,' and it was evident that, in spite of the instructions which he had given me as to the disposal of Alresca, Toddy was claiming the patient for his own. I retired. It was the only thing I could do. Two doctors were not needed, and I did not see myself, a young man scarcely yet escaped from the fear of examinations, disputing cases with the redoubtable Toddy. I heard afterwards that he had prolonged his stay in London in order to attend Alresca. So that I had not seen the tenor since his accident.

"What does Monsieur Alresca want to see me about?" I demanded cautiously.

"He will tell you," said Rosa, equally cautious.

A silence followed.

"Do you think I upset him—that night?" she asked.

"You wish me to be frank?"

"If I had thought you would not be frank I would not have asked you. Do you imagine it is my habit to go about putting awkward questions like that?"

"I think you did upset him very much."

"You think I was wrong?"

"I do."

"Perhaps you are right," she admitted.

I had been bold. A desire took me to be still bolder. She was in the carriage with me. She was not older than I. And were she Rosetta Rosa, or a mere miss taken at hazard out of a drawing-room, she was feminine and I was masculine. In short—Well, I have fits of rashness sometimes.

"You say he is depressed," I addressed her firmly. "And I will venture to inform you that I am not in the least surprised."

"Oh!" she exclaimed. "And why?"

"After what you said to him that night in the dressing-room. If I had been in Alresca's place I know that I should be depressed, and very much depressed, too."

"You mean—" she faltered.

"Yes," I said, "I mean that."

I thought I had gone pretty far, and my heart was beating. I could not justly have protested had she stopped the carriage and deposited me on the pavement by the railings of Green Park. But her character was angelic. She accepted my treatment of her with the most astounding meekness.

"You mean," she said, "that he is in love with me, and I chose just that night to—refuse him."

I nodded.

"That is emotional cause enough, isn't it, to account for any mysterious depression that any man is ever likely to have?"

"You are mistaken," she said softly. "You don't know Alresca. You don't know his strength of mind. I can assure you that it is something more than unreturned love that is destroying him."

"Destroying him?"

"Yes, destroying him. Alresca is capable of killing a futile passion. His soul is too far removed from his body, and even from his mind, to be seriously influenced by the mistakes and misfortunes of his mind and body. Do you understand me?"

"I think so."

"What is the matter with Alresca is something in his most secret soul."

"And you can form no idea of what it is?"

She made no reply.

"Doctors certainly can't cure such diseases as that," I said.

"They can try," said Rosetta Rosa.

"You wish me to try?" I faced her.

She inclined her head.

"Then I will," I said with sudden passionateness, forgetting even that I was not Alresca's doctor.

The carriage stopped. In the space of less than a quarter of an hour, so it seemed to me, we had grown almost intimate—she and I.

Alresca's man was awaiting us in the portico of the Devonshire, and without a word he led us to his master. Alresca lay on his back on a couch in a large and luxuriously littered drawing-room. The pallor of his face and the soft brilliance of his eyes were infinitely pathetic, and again he reminded me of the tragic and gloomy third act of "Tristan." He greeted us kindly in his quiet voice.

"I have brought the young man," said Rosa, "and now, after I have inquired about your health, I must go. It is late. Are you better, Alresca?"

"I am better now that you are here," he smiled. "But you must not go yet. It is many days since I heard a note of music. Sing to me before you go."

"To-night?"

"Yes, to-night."

"What shall I sing?"

"Anything, so that I hear your voice."

"I will sing 'Elsa's Dream.' But who will accompany? You know I simply can't play to my own singing."

I gathered together all my courage.

"I'm an awful player," I said, "but I know the whole score of *Lohengrin*."

"How clever of you!" Rosa laughed. "I'm sure you play beautifully."

Alresca rewarded me with a look, and, trembling, I sat down to the piano. I was despicably nervous. Before the song was finished I had lost everything but honour; but I played that accompaniment to the most marvellous soprano in the world.

And what singing! Rosa stood close beside me. I caught the golden voice at its birth. Every vibration, every shade of expression, every subtlety of feeling was mine; and the experience was unforgettable.

Many times since then have I heard Rosa sing, many times in my hearing has she excited a vast audience to overwhelming enthusiasm; but never, to my mind, has she sung so finely as on that night. She was profoundly moved, she had in Alresca the ideal listener, and she sang with the magic power of a goddess. It was the summit of her career.

"There is none like you," Alresca said, and the praise of Alresca brought the crimson to her cheek. He was probably the one person living who had the right to praise her, for an artist can only be properly estimated by his equals.

"Come to me, Rosa," he murmured, as he took her hand in his and kissed it. "You are in exquisite voice to-night," he said.

"Am I?"

"Yes. You have been excited; and I notice that you always sing best under excitement."

"Perhaps," she replied. "The fact is, I have just met—met someone whom I never expected to meet. That is all. Good night, dear friend."

"Good night."

She passed her hand soothingly over his forehead.

When we were alone Alresca seemed to be overtaken by lassitude.

"Surely," I said, "it is not by Toddy—I mean Dr Todhunter MacWhirter's advice that you keep these hours. The clocks are striking two!"

"Ah, my friend," he replied wearily, in his precise and rather elaborate English, "ill or well, I must live as I have been accustomed to live. For twenty years I have gone to bed promptly at three o'clock and risen at eleven o'clock. Must I change because of a broken thigh? In an hour's time, and not before, my people will carry this couch and its burden to my bedroom. Then I shall pretend to sleep; but I shall not sleep. Somehow of late the habit of sleep has left me. Hitherto, I have scorned opiates, which are the refuge of the weak-minded, yet I fear I may be compelled to ask you for one. There was a time when I could will myself to sleep. But not now, not now!"

"I am not your medical adviser," I said, mindful of professional etiquette, "and I could not think of administering an opiate without the express permission of Dr MacWhirter."

"Pardon me," he said, his eyes resting on me with a quiet satisfaction that touched me to the heart, "but you are my medical adviser, if you will honour me so far. I have not forgotten your neat hand and skilful treatment of me at the time of my accident. To-day the little Scotchman told me that my thigh was progressing quite admirably, and that all I needed was nursing. I suggested to him that you should finish the case. He had, in fact, praised your skill. And so, Mr Foster, will you be my doctor? I want you to examine me thoroughly, for, unless I deceive myself, I am suffering from some mysterious complaint."

I was enormously, ineffably flattered and delighted, and all the boy in me wanted to caper around the room and then to fall on Alresca's neck and dissolve in gratitude to him. But instead of these feats, I put on a vast seriousness (which must really have been very funny to behold), and then I thanked Alresca in formal phrases, and then, quite in the correct professional style, I began to make gentle fun of his idea of a mysterious complaint, and I asked him for a catalogue of his symptoms. I perceived that he and Rosa must have previously arranged that I should be requested to become his doctor.

"There are no symptoms," he replied, "except a gradual loss of vitality. But examine me."

I did so most carefully, testing the main organs, and subjecting him to a severe cross-examination.

"Well?" he said, as, after I had finished, I sat down to cogitate.

"Well, Monsieur Alresca, all I can say is that your fancy is too lively. That is what you suffer from, an excitable fan—"

"Stay, my friend," he interrupted me with a firm gesture. "Before you go any further, let me entreat you to be frank. Without absolute candour nothing can be done. I think I am a tolerable judge of faces, and I can read in yours the fact that my condition has puzzled you."

I paused, taken aback. It had puzzled me. I thought of all that Rosetta Rosa had said, and I hesitated. Then I made up my mind.

"I yield," I responded. "You are not an ordinary man, and it was absurd of me to treat you as one. Absolute candour is, as you say, essential, and so I'll confess that your case does puzzle me. There is no organic disease, but there is a quite unaccountable organic weakness—a weakness which fifty broken thighs would not explain. I must observe, and endeavour to discover the cause. In the meantime I have only one piece of advice. You know that in certain cases we have to tell women patients that a successful issue depends on their own willpower: I say the same thing to you."

"Receive my thanks," he said. "You have acted as I hoped. As for the willpower, that is another matter," and a faint smile crossed his handsome, melancholy face.

I rose to leave. It was nearly three o'clock.

"Give me a few moments longer. I have a favour to ask."

After speaking these words he closed his eyes, as though to recall the opening sentences of a carefully prepared speech.

"I am entirely at your service," I murmured.

"Mr Foster," he began, "you are a young man of brilliant accomplishments, at the commencement of your career. Doubtless you have made your plans for the immediate future, and I feel quite sure that those plans do not include any special attendance upon myself, whom until the other day you had never met. I am a stranger to you, and on the part of a stranger it would be presumptuous to ask you to alter your plans. Nevertheless, I am at this moment capable of that presumption. In my life I have not often made requests, but such requests as I have made have never been refused. I hope that my good fortune in this respect may continue. Mr Foster, I wish to leave England. I wish to die in my own place—"

I shrugged my shoulders in protest against the word 'die.'

"If you prefer it, I wish to live in my own place. Will you accompany me as companion? I am convinced that we should suit each other—that I should derive benefit from your skill and pleasure from your society, while you—you would tolerate the whims and eccentricities of my middle age. We need not discuss terms; you would merely name your fee."

There was, as a matter of fact, no reason in the world why I should have agreed to this suggestion of Alresca's. As he himself had said, we were strangers, and I was under no obligation to him of any kind.

Yet at once I felt an impulse to accept his proposal. Whence that impulse sprang I cannot say. Perhaps from the aspect of an adventure that the affair had. Perhaps from the vague idea that by attaching myself to Alresca I should be brought again into contact with Rosetta Rosa. Certainly I admired him immensely. None who knew him could avoid doing so. Already, indeed, I had for him a feeling akin to affection.

"I see by your face," he said, "that you are not altogether unwilling. You accept?"

"With pleasure;" and I smiled with the pleasure I felt.

But it seemed to me that I gave the answer independently of my own volition. The words were uttered almost before I knew.

"It is very good of you."

"Not at all," I said. "I have made no plans, and therefore nothing will be disarranged. Further, I count it an honour; and, moreover, your 'case'—pardon the word—interests me deeply. Where do you wish to go?"

"To Bruges, of course."

He seemed a little surprised that I should ask the question.

"Bruges," he went on, "that dear and wonderful old city of Flanders, is the place of my birth. You have visited it?"

"No," I said, "but I have often heard that it is the most picturesque city in Europe, and I should like to see it awfully."

"There is nothing in the world like Bruges," he said. "Bruges the Dead they call it; a fit spot in which to die."

"If you talk like that I shall reconsider my decision."

"Pardon, pardon!" he laughed, suddenly wearing an appearance of gaiety. "I am happier now. When can we go? To-morrow? Let it be to-morrow."

"Impossible," I said. "The idea of a man whose thigh was broken less than a fortnight since taking a sea voyage to-morrow! Do you know that under the most favourable circumstances it will be another five or six weeks before the bone unites, and that even then the greatest care will be necessary?"

His gaiety passed.

"Five more weeks here?"

"I fear so."

"But our agreement shall come into operation at once. You will visit me daily? Rather, you will live here?"

"If it pleases you. I am sure I shall be charmed to live here."

"Let the time go quickly—let it fly! Ah, Mr Foster, you will like Bruges. It is the most dignified of cities. It has the picturesqueness of Nuremburg, the waterways of Amsterdam, the squares of Turin, the monuments of Perugia, the cafés of Florence, and the smells of Cologne. I have an old house there of the seventeenth century; it is on the Quai des Augustins."

"A family affair?" I questioned.

"No; I bought it only a few years ago from a friend. I fear I cannot boast of much family. My mother made lace, my father was a schoolmaster. They are both dead, and I have no relatives."

Somewhere in the building a clock struck three, and at that instant there was a tap at the door, and Alresca's valet discreetly entered.

"Monsieur rang?"

"No, Alexis. Leave us."

Comprehending that it was at last Alresca's hour for retiring, I rose to leave, and called the man back.

"Good night, dear friend," said Alresca, pressing my hand. "I shall expect you to-morrow, and in the meantime a room shall be prepared for you. *Au revoir.*"

Alexis conducted me to the door. As he opened it he made a civil remark about the beauty of the night. I glanced at his face.

"You *are* English, aren't you?" I asked him.

"Yes, sir."

"I only ask because Alexis is such a peculiar name for an Englishman."

"It is merely a name given to me by Monsieur Alresca when I entered his service several years ago. My name is John Smedley."

"Well, Mr Smedley," I said, putting half a sovereign into his hand, "I perceive that you are a man of intelligence."

"Hope so, sir."

"I am a doctor, and to-morrow, as I dare say you heard, I am coming to live here with your master in order to attend him medically."

"Yes, sir."

"He says he is suffering from some mysterious complaint, Smedley."

"He told me as much, sir."

"Do you know what that complaint is?"

"Haven't the least idea, sir. But he always seems low like, and he gets lower, especially during the nights. What might the complaint be, sir?"

"I wish I could tell you. By the way, haven't you had trained nurses there?"

"Yes, sir. The other doctor sent two. But the governor dismissed 'em yesterday. He told me they worried him. Me and the butler does what's necessary."

"You say he is more depressed during the nights—you mean he shows the effects of that depression in the mornings?"

"Just so, sir."

"I am going to be confidential, Smedley. Are you aware if your master has any secret trouble on his mind, any worry that he reveals to no one?"

"No, sir, I am not."

"Thank you, Smedley. Good night."

"Good night, sir, and thank *you*."

I had obtained no light from Alexis, and I sought in vain for an explanation of my patient's condition. Of course, it was plausible enough to argue that his passion for Rosa was at the root of the evil; but I remembered Rosa's words to me in the carriage, and I was disposed to agree with them. To me, as to her, it seemed that, though Alresca was the sort of man to love deeply, he was not the sort of man to allow an attachment, however profound or unfortunate, to make a wreck of his existence. No. If Alresca was dying, he was not dying of love.

As Alexis had remarked, it was a lovely summer night, and after quitting the Devonshire I stood idly on the pavement, and gazed about me in simple enjoyment of the scene.

The finest trees in Hyde Park towered darkly in front of me, and above them was spread the star-strewn sky, with a gibbous moon just showing over the housetops to the left. I could not see a soul, but faintly from the distance came the tramp of a policeman on his beat. The hour, to my busy fancy, seemed full of fate. But it was favourable to meditation, and I thought, and thought, and thought. Was I at the beginning of an adventure, or would the business, so strangely initiated, resolve itself into something prosaic and mediocre? I had a suspicion—indeed, I had a hope—that adventures were in store for me. Perhaps peril also. For the sinister impression originally made upon me by that ridiculous crystal-gazing scene into which I had been entrapped by Emmeline had returned, and do what I would I could not dismiss it.

My cousin's wife was sincere, with all her vulgarity and inborn snobbishness. And that being assumed, how did I stand with regard to Rosetta Rosa? Was the thing a coincidence, or had I indeed crossed her path pursuant to some strange decree of Fate—a decree which Emmeline had divined or guessed or presaged? There was a certain weirdness about Emmeline that was rather puzzling.

I had seen Rosa but twice, and her image, to use the old phrase, was stamped on my heart. True! Yet the heart of any young man who had talked with Rosa twice would in all probability have been similarly affected. Rosa was not the ordinary pretty and clever girl. She was such a creature as grows in this world not often in a century. She was an angel out of Paradise—an angel who might pass across Europe and leave behind her a trail of broken hearts to mark the transit. And if angels could sing as she did, then no wonder that the heavenly choirs were happy in nothing but song. (You are to remember that it was three o'clock in the morning.) No, the fact that I was already half in love with Rosa proved nothing.

On the other hand, might not the manner in which she and Alresca had sought me out be held to prove something? Why should such exalted personages think twice about a mere student of medicine who had had the good fortune once to make himself useful at a critical juncture? Surely, I could argue that here was the hand of Fate.

Rubbish! I was an ass to stand there at that unearthly hour, robbing myself of sleep in order to pursue such trains of thought. Besides, supposing that Rosa and myself were, in fact, drawn together by chance or fate, or whatever you like to call it, had not disaster been prophesied in that event? It would be best to leave the future alone. My aim should be to cure Alresca, and then go soberly to Totnes and join my brother in practice.

I turned down Oxford Street, whose perspective of gas-lamps stretched east and west to distances apparent infinite, and as I did so I suddenly knew that someone was standing by the railings opposite, under the shadow of the great trees. I had been so sure that I was alone that this discovery startled me a little, and I began to whistle tunelessly.

I could make out no details of the figure, except that it was a man who stood there, and to satisfy my curiosity I went across to inspect him. To my astonishment he was very well, though very quietly, dressed, and had the appearance of being a gentleman of the highest distinction. His face was clean-shaven, and I noticed the fine, firm chin, and the clear, unblinking eyes. He stood quite still, and as I approached looked me full in the face. It was a terrible gaze, and I do not mind confessing that, secretly, I quailed under it; there was malice and a dangerous hate in that gaze. Nevertheless I was young, careless, and enterprising.

"Can you tell me if I am likely to get a cab at this time of night?" I asked as lightly as I could. I wanted to hear his voice.

But he returned no answer, merely gazing at me as before, without a movement.

"Strange!" I said, half to myself. "The fellow must be deaf, or mad, or a foreigner."

The man smiled slightly, his lips drooping to a sneer. I retreated, and as I stepped back on the curb my foot touched some small object. I looked down, and in the dim light, for the dawn was already heralded, I saw the glitter of jewels. I stooped and picked the thing up. It was the same little dagger which but a few hours before I had seen Rosa present with so much formality to Sir Cyril Smart. But there was this difference—the tiny blade was covered with blood!

VI

ALRESCA'S FATE

THE HOUSE WAS LARGE, AND its beautiful façade fronted a narrow canal. To say that the spot was picturesque is to say little, for the whole of Bruges is picturesque. This corner of the Quai des Augustins was distinguished even in Bruges. The aspect of the mansion, with its wide entrance and broad courtyard, on which the inner windows looked down in regular array, was simple and dignified in the highest degree. The architecture was an entirely admirable specimen of Flemish domestic work of the best period, and the internal decoration and the furniture matched to a nicety the exterior. It was in that grave and silent abode, with Alresca, that I first acquired a taste for bric-à-brac. Ah! the Dutch marquetry, the French cabinetry, the Belgian brassware, the curious panellings, the oak-frames, the faience, the silver candlesticks, the Amsterdam toys in silver, the Antwerp incunables, and the famous tenth-century illuminated manuscript in half-uncials! Such trifles abounded, and in that antique atmosphere they had the quality of exquisite fitness.

And on the greenish waters of the canal floated several gigantic swans, with insatiable and endless appetites. We used to feed them from the dining-room windows, which overhung the canal.

I was glad to be out of London, and as the days passed my gladness increased. I had not been pleased with myself in London. As the weeks followed each other, I had been compelled to admit to myself that the case of Alresca held mysteries for me, even medical mysteries. During the first day or two I had thought that I understood it, and I had despised the sayings of Rosetta Rosa in the carriage, and the misgivings with which my original examination of Alresca had inspired me. And then I gradually perceived that, after all, the misgivings had been justified. The man's thigh made due progress; but the man, slowly failing, lost interest in the struggle for life.

Here I might proceed to a technical dissertation upon his physical state, but it would be useless. A cloud of long words will not cover ignorance; and I was most emphatically ignorant. At least, such knowledge as I had obtained was merely of a negative character. All that I could be sure of was that this was by no means an instance of mysterious disease. There was no disease, as we understand the term. In particular, there was no decay of the nerve-centres. Alresca was well—in good health. What he lacked was the will to live—that strange and mystic impulse which alone divides us from death. It was, perhaps, hard on a young G.P. to be confronted by such a medical conundrum at the very outset of his career; but, then, the Maker of conundrums seldom considers the age and inexperience of those who are requested to solve them.

Yes, this was the first practical proof that had come to me of the sheer empiricism of the present state of medicine.

We had lived together—Alresca and I—peaceably, quietly, sadly. He appeared to have ample means, and the standard of luxury which existed in his flat was a high one. He was a connoisseur in every department of art and life, and took care that he was well served. Perhaps it would be more correct to say that he had once taken care to be well served, and that the custom primarily established went on by its own momentum. For he did not exercise even such control as a sick man might have been expected to exercise. He seemed to be concerned with nothing, save that occasionally he would exhibit a flickering curiosity as to the opera season which was drawing to a close.

Unfortunately, there was little operatic gossip to be curious about. Rosa had fulfilled her engagement and gone to another capital, and since her departure the season had, perhaps inevitably, fallen flat. Of course, the accident to and indisposition of Alresca had also contributed to this end. And there had been another factor in the case—a factor which, by the way, constituted the sole item of news capable of rousing Alresca from his torpor. I refer to the disappearance of Sir Cyril Smart.

Soon after my cousin Sullivan's reception, the papers had reported Sir Cyril to be ill, and then it was stated that he had retired to a remote Austrian watering-place (name unmentioned) in order to rest and recuperate. Certain weekly papers of the irresponsible sort gave publicity to queer rumors—that Sir Cyril had fought a duel and been wounded, that he had been attacked one night in the streets, even that he was dead. But these rumors were generally discredited, and meanwhile the opera season ran its course under the guidance of Sir Cyril's head man, Mr Nolan, so famous for his diamond shirt-stud.

Perhaps I could have thrown some light upon the obscurity which enveloped the doings of Sir Cyril Smart. But I preferred to remain inactive. Locked away in my writing-case I kept the jewelled dagger so mysteriously found by me outside the Devonshire Mansion.

I had mentioned the incidents of that night to no one, and probably not a soul on the planet guessed that the young doctor in attendance upon Alresca had possession of a little toy-weapon which formed a startling link between two existences supposed to be unconnected save in the way of business—those of Sir Cyril and Rosetta Rosa. I hesitated whether to send the dagger to Rosa, and finally decided that I would wait until I saw her again, if ever that should happen, and then do as circumstances should dictate. I often wondered whether the silent man with the fixed gaze, whom I had met in Oxford Street that night, had handled the dagger, or whether his presence was a mere coincidence. To my speculations I discovered no answer.

Then the moment had come when Alresca's thigh was so far mended that, under special conditions, we could travel, and one evening, after a journey full of responsibilities for me, we had arrived in Bruges.

Soon afterwards came a slight alteration.

Alresca took pleasure in his lovely house, and I was aware of an improvement in his condition. The torpor was leaving him, and his spirits grew livelier. Unfortunately, it was difficult to give him outdoor exercise, since the roughly paved streets made driving impossible for him, and he was far from being able to walk. After a time I contrived to hire a large rowing boat, and on fine afternoons it was our custom to lower him from the quay among the swans into this somewhat unwieldy craft, so that he might take the air as a Venetian. The idea tickled him, and our progress along the disused canals was always a matter of interest to the townspeople, who showed an unappeasable inquisitiveness concerning their renowned fellow citizen.

It was plain to me that he was recovering; that he had lifted himself out of the circle of that strange influence under which he had nearly parted with his life. The fact was plain to me, but the explanation of the fact was not plain. I was as much puzzled by his rise as I had been puzzled by his descent. But that did not prevent me from trying to persuade myself that this felicitous change in my patient's state must be due, after all, to the results of careful dieting, a proper curriculum of daily existence, supervision of mental tricks and habits—in short, of all that minute care and solicitude which only a resident doctor can give to a sick man.

One evening he was especially alert and gay, and I not less so. We were in the immense drawing-room, which, like the dining-room, overlooked the canal. Dinner was finished—we dined at six, the Bruges hour—and Alresca lay on his invalid's couch, ejecting from his mouth rings of the fine blue smoke of a Javanese cigar, a box of which I had found at the tobacco shop kept by two sisters at the corner of the Grande Place. I stood at the great central window, which was wide open, and watched the whiteness of the swans moving vaguely over the surface of the canal in the oncoming twilight. The air was warm and heavy, and the long, high-pitched whine of the mosquito swarms—sole pest of the city—had already begun.

"Alresca," I said, "your days as an invalid are numbered."

"Why do you say that?"

"No one who was really an invalid could possibly enjoy that cigar as you are enjoying it."

"A good cigar—a glass of good wine," he murmured, savouring the perfume of the cigar. "What would life be without them?"

"A few weeks ago, and you would have said: 'What is life even with them?'"

"Then you really think I am better?" he smiled.

"I'm sure of it."

"As for me," he returned, "I confess it. That has happened which I thought never would happen. I am once more interested in life. The wish to live has come back. I am glad to be alive. Carl, your first case has been a success."

"No thanks to me," I said. "Beyond seeing that you didn't displace the broken pieces of your thigh-bone, what have I done? Nothing. No one knows that better than you do."

"That's your modesty—your incurable modesty."

I shook my head, and went to stand by his couch. I was profoundly aware then, despite all the efforts of my self-conceit to convince myself to the contrary, that I had effected nothing whatever towards his recovery, that it had accomplished itself without external aid. But that did not lessen my intense pleasure in the improvement. By this time I had a most genuine affection for Alresca. The rare qualities of the man—his serenity, his sense of justice, his invariable politeness and consideration, the pureness of his soul—had captured me completely. I was his friend. Perhaps I was his best friend in the world. The singular circumstances of our coming together had helped much to strengthen the tie between us. I glanced down at him, full of my affection for him, and minded to take advantage of the rights of that affection for once in a way.

"Alresca," I said quietly.

"Well?"

"What was it?"

"What was what?"

I met his gaze.

"What was that thing that you have fought and driven off? What is the mystery of it? You know—you must know. Tell me."

His eyelids fell.

"Better to leave the past alone," said he. "Granting that I had formed an idea, I could not put it into proper words. I have tried to do so. In the expectation of death I wrote down certain matters. But these I shall now destroy. I am wiser, less morbid. I can perceive that there are fields of thought of which it is advisable to keep closed the gates. Do as I do, Carl—forget. Take the credit for my recovery, and be content with that."

I felt that he was right, and resumed my position near the window, humming a tune.

"In a week you may put your foot to the ground; you will then no longer have to be carried about like a parcel." I spoke in a casual tone.

"Good!" he ejaculated.

"And then our engagement will come to an end, and you will begin to sing again."

"Ah!" he said contemplatively, after a pause, "sing!"

It seemed as if singing was a different matter.

"Yes," I repeated, "sing. You must throw yourself into that. It will be the best of all tonics."

"Have I not told you that I should never sing again?"

"Perhaps you have," I replied; "but I don't remember. And even if you have, as you yourself have just said, you are now wiser, less morbid."

"True!" he murmured. "Yes, I must sing. They want me at Chicago. I will go, and while there I will spread abroad the fame of Carl Foster."

He smiled gaily, and then his face became meditative and sad.

"My artistic career has never been far away from tragedy," he said at length. "It was founded on a tragedy, and not long ago I thought it would end in one."

I waited in silence, knowing that if he wished to tell me any private history, he would begin of his own accord.

"You are listening, Carl?"

I nodded. It was growing dusk.

"You remember I pointed out to you the other day the little house in the Rue d'Ostende where my parents lived?"

"Perfectly."

"That," he proceeded, using that curiously formal and elaborate English which he must have learned from reading books, "that was the scene of the tragedy which made me an artist. I have told you that my father was a schoolmaster. He was the kindest of men, but he had moods of frightful severity—moods which subsided as quickly as they arose. At the age of three, just as I was beginning to talk easily, I became, for a period, subject to fits; and in one of these I lost the power of speech. I, Alresca, could make no sound; and for seven years that tenor whom in the future people were to call 'golden-throated,' and 'world-famous,' and 'unrivalled,' had no voice." He made a deprecatory gesture. "When I think of it, Carl, I can scarcely believe it—so strange are the chances of life. I could hear and understand, but I could not speak.

"Of course, that was forty years ago, and the system of teaching mutes to talk was not then invented, or, at any rate, not generally understood. So I was known and pitied as the poor dumb boy. I took pleasure in dumb animals, and had for pets a silver-grey cat, a goat, and a little spaniel. One afternoon—I should be about ten years old—my father came home from his school and sitting down, laid his head on the table and began to cry. Seeing him cry, I also began to cry; I was acutely sensitive.

"'What is the matter?' asked my good mother.

"'Alas!' he said, 'I am a murderer!'

"'Nay, that cannot be,' she replied.

"'I say it is so,' said my father. 'I have murdered a child—a little girl. I grumbled at her yesterday. I was annoyed and angry—because she had done her lessons ill. I sent her home, but instead of going home she went to the outer canal and drowned herself. They came and told me this afternoon. Yes, I am a murderer!'

"I howled, while my mother tried to comfort my father, pointing out to him that if he had spoken roughly to the child it was done for the child's good, and that he could not possibly have foreseen the catastrophe. But her words were in vain.

"We all went to bed. In the middle of the night I heard my dear silver-grey cat mewing at the back of the house. She had been locked out. I rose and went down-stairs to let her in. To do so it was necessary for me to pass through the kitchen. It was quite dark, and I knocked against something in the darkness. With an inarticulate scream, I raced up-stairs again to my parents' bedroom. I seized my mother by her night-dress and dragged her towards the door. She stopped only to light a candle, and hand-in-hand we went down-stairs to the kitchen. The candle threw around its fitful, shuddering glare, and my mother's eyes followed mine. Some strange thing happened in my throat.

"'Mother!' I cried, in a hoarse, uncouth, horrible voice, and, casting myself against her bosom, I clung convulsively to her. From a hook in the ceiling beam my father's corpse dangled. He had hanged himself in the frenzy of his remorse. So my speech came to me again."

All the man's genius for tragic acting, that genius which had made him unique in *Tristan* and in *Tannhauser*, had been displayed in this recital; and its solitary auditor was more moved by it than superficially appeared. Neither of us spoke a word for a few minutes. Then Alresca, taking aim, threw the end of his cigar out of the window.

"Yes," I said at length, "that was tragedy, that was!"

He proceeded:

"The critics are always praising me for the emotional qualities in my singing. Well, I cannot use my voice without thinking of the dreadful circumstance under which Fate saw fit to restore that which Fate had taken away."

And there fell a long silence, and night descended on the canal, and the swans were nothing now but pale ghosts wandering soundlessly over the water.

"Carl," Alresca burst out with a start—he was decidedly in a mood to be communicative that evening—"have you ever been in love?"

In the gloom I could just distinguish that he was leaning his head on his arm.

"No," I answered; "at least, I think not;" and I wondered if I had been, if I was, in love.

"You have that which pleases women, you know, and you will have chances, plenty of chances. Let me advise you—either fall in love young or not at all. If you have a disappointment before you are twenty-five it is nothing. If you have a disappointment after you are thirty-five, it is—everything."

He sighed.

"No, Alresca," I said, surmising that he referred to his own case, "not everything, surely?"

"You are right," he replied. "Even then it is not everything. The human soul is unconquerable, even by love. But, nevertheless, be warned. Do not drive it late. Ah! Why should I not confess to you, now that all is over? Carl, you are aware that I have loved deeply. Can you guess what being in love meant to me? Probably not. I am aging now, but in my youth I was handsome, and I have had my voice. Women, the richest, the cleverest, the kindest—they fling themselves at such as me. There is no vanity in saying so; it is the simple fact. I might have married a hundred times; I might have been loved a thousand times. But I remained—as I was. My heart slept like that of a young girl. I rejected alike the open advances of the bold and the shy, imperceptible signals of the timid. Women were not for me. In secret I despised them. I really believe I did.

"Then—and it is not yet two years ago—I met her whom you know. And I—I the scorner, fell in love. All my pride, my self-assurance crumbled into ruin about me, and left me naked to the torment of an unrequited passion. I could not credit the depth of my misfortune, and at first it was impossible for me to believe that she was serious in refusing me. But she had the right. She was an angel, and I only a man. She was the most beautiful woman in the world."

"She was—she is," I said.

He laughed easily.

"She is," he repeated. "But she is nothing to me. I admire her beauty and her goodness, that is all. She refused me. Good! At first I rebelled against my fate, then I accepted it." And he repeated: "Then I accepted it."

I might have made some reply to his flattering confidences, but I heard someone walk quickly across the foot-path outside and through the wide entrance porch. In another moment the door of the salon was

thrown open, and a figure stood radiant and smiling in the doorway. The
antechamber had already been lighted, and the figure was silhouetted
against the yellow radiance.

"So you are here, and I have found you, all in the dark!"

Alresca turned his head.

"Rosa!" he cried in bewilderment, put out his arms, and then drew
them sharply back again.

It was Rosetta. She ran towards us, and shook hands with kind expressions
of greeting, and our eyes followed her as she moved about, striking matches
and applying them to candles. Then she took off her hat and veil.

"There! I seemed to know the house," she said. "Immediately I had
entered the courtyard I felt that there was a corridor running to the
right, and at the end of that corridor some steps and a landing and a
door, and on the other side of that door a large drawing-room. And so,
without ringing or waiting for the faithful Alexis, I came in."

"And what brings you to Bruges, dear lady?" asked Alresca.

"Solicitude for your health, dear sir," she replied, smiling. "At
Bayreuth I met that quaint person, Mrs Sullivan Smith, who told me
that you were still here with Mr Foster; and to-day, as I was travelling
from Cologne to Ostend, the idea suddenly occurred to me to spend
one night at Bruges, and make inquiries into your condition—and
that of Mr Foster. You know the papers have been publishing the most
contradictory accounts."

"Have they indeed?" laughed Alresca.

But I could see that he was nervous and not at ease. For myself, I was,
it must be confessed, enchanted to see Rosa again, and so unexpectedly,
and it was amazingly nice of her to include myself in her inquiries, and
yet I divined that it would have been better if she had never come. I
had a sense of some sort of calamity.

Alresca was flushed. He spoke in short, hurried sentences. Alternately
his tones were passionate and studiously cold. Rosa's lovely presence,
her musical chatter, her gay laughter, filled the room. She seemed to
exhale a delightful and intoxicating atmosphere, which spread itself
through the chamber and enveloped the soul of Alresca. It was as if he

fought against an influence, and then gradually yielded to the sweetness of it. I observed him closely—for was he not my patient?—and I guessed that a struggle was passing within him. I thought of what he had just been saying to me, and I feared lest the strong will should be scarcely so strong as it had deemed itself.

"You have dined?" asked Alresca.

"I have eaten," she said. "One does not dine after a day's travelling."

"Won't you have some coffee?"

She consented to the coffee, which Alexis John Smedley duly brought in, and presently she was walking lightly to and fro, holding the tiny white cup in her white hand, and peering at the furniture and bric-à-brac by the light of several candles. Between whiles she related to Alresca all the news of their operatic acquaintances—how this one was married, another stranded in Buenos Ayres, another ill with jealousy, another ill with a cold, another pursued for debt, and so on through the diverting category.

"And Smart?" Alresca queried at length.

I had been expecting and hoping for this question.

"Oh, Sir Cyril! I have heard nothing of him. He is not a person that interests me."

She shut her lips tight and looked suddenly across in my direction, and our eyes met, but she made no sign that I could interpret. If she had known that the little jewelled dagger lay in the room over her head!

Her straw hat and thin white veil lay on a settee between two windows. She picked them up, and began to pull the pins out of the hat. Then she put the hat down again.

"I must run away soon, Alresca," she said, bending over him, "but before I leave I should like to go through the whole house. It seems such a quaint place. Will you let Mr Foster show me? He shall not be away from you long."

"In the dark?"

"Why not? We can have candles."

And so, a heavy silver candlestick in either hand, I presently found myself preceding Rosa up the wide branching staircase of the house. We had left the owner with a reading-lamp at the head of his couch, and a copy of *Madame Bovary* to pass the time.

We stopped at the first landing to examine a picture.

"That mysterious complaint that he had, or thought he had, in London has left him, has it not?" she asked me suddenly, in a low, slightly apprehensive, confidential tone, moving her head in the direction of the salon below.

For some reason I hesitated.

"He says so," I replied cautiously. "At any rate, he is much better."

"Yes, I can see that. But he is still in a very nervous condition."

"Ah," I said, "that is only—only at certain times."

As we went together from room to room I forgot everything except the fact of her presence. Never was beauty so powerful as hers; never was the power of beauty used so artlessly, with such a complete unconsciousness. I began gloomily to speculate on the chances of her ultimately marrying Alresca, and a remark from her awoke me from my abstraction. We were nearing the top of the house.

"It is all familiar to me, in a way," she said.

"Why, you said the same downstairs. Have you been here before?"

"Never, to my knowledge."

We were traversing a long, broad passage side by side. Suddenly I tripped over an unexpected single stair, and nearly fell. Rosa, however, had allowed for it.

"I didn't see that step," I said.

"Nor I," she answered, "but I knew, somehow, that it was there. It is very strange and uncanny, and I shall insist on an explanation from Alresca." She gave a forced laugh.

As I fumbled with the handle of the door she took hold of my hand.

"Listen!" she said excitedly, "this will be a small room, and over the mantelpiece is a little round picture of a dog."

I opened the door with something akin to a thrill. This part of the house was unfamiliar to me. The room was certainly a small one, but there was no little round picture over the mantelpiece. It was a square picture, and rather large, and a sea-piece.

"You guessed wrong," I said, and I felt thankful.

"No, no, I am sure."

She went to the square picture, and lifted it away from the wall.

"Look!" she said.

Behind the picture was a round whitish mark on the wall, showing where another picture had previously hung.

"Let us go, let us go! I don't like the flicker of these candles," she murmured, and she seized my arm.

We returned to the corridor. Her grip of me tightened.

"Was not that Alresca?" she cried.

"Where?"

"At the end of the corridor—there!"

"I saw no one, and it couldn't have been he, for the simple reason that he can't walk yet, not to mention climbing three flights of stairs. You have made yourself nervous."

We descended to the ground-floor. In the main hall Alresca's housekeeper, evidently an old acquaintance, greeted Rosa with a curtsy, and she stopped to speak to the woman. I went on to the salon.

The aspect of the room is vividly before me now as I write. Most of the great chamber was in a candle-lit gloom, but the reading-lamp burnt clearly at the head of the couch, throwing into prominence the fine profile of Alresca's face. He had fallen asleep, or at any rate his eyes were closed. The copy of *Madame Bovary* lay on the floor, and near it a gold pencil-case. Quietly I picked the book up, and saw on the yellow cover of it some words written in pencil. These were the words:

"Carl, I love her. He has come again. This time it is—"

I looked long at his calm and noble face, and bent and listened. At that moment Rosa entered. Concealing the book, I held out my right hand with a gesture.

"Softly!" I enjoined her, and my voice broke.

"Why? What?"

"He is dead," I said.

It did not occur to me that I ought to have prepared her.

VII

THE VIGIL BY THE BIER

WE LOOKED AT EACH OTHER, Rosa and I, across the couch of Alresca.

All the vague and terrible apprehensions, disquietudes, misgivings, which the gradual improvement in Alresca's condition had lulled to sleep, aroused themselves again in my mind, coming, as it were, boldly out into the open from the dark, unexplored grottos wherein they had crouched and hidden. And I went back in memory to those sinister days in London before I had brought Alresca to Bruges, days over which a mysterious horror had seemed to brood.

I felt myself adrift in a sea of frightful suspicions. I remembered Alresca's delirium on the night of his accident, and his final hallucination concerning the blank wall in the dressing-room (if hallucination it was), also on that night. I remembered his outburst against Rosetta Rosa. I remembered Emmeline Smith's outburst against Rosetta Rosa. I remembered the vision in the crystal, and Rosa's sudden and astoundingly apt breaking in upon that vision. I remembered the scene between Rosa and Sir Cyril Smart, and her almost hysterical impulse to pierce her own arm with the little jewelled dagger. I remembered the glint of the dagger which drew my attention to it on the curb of an Oxford Street pavement afterwards. I remembered the disappearance of Sir Cyril Smart. I remembered all the inexplicable circumstances of Alresca's strange decay, and his equally strange recovery. I remembered that his recovery had coincided with an entire absence of communication between himself and Rosa … And then she comes! And within an hour he is dead! "I love her. He has come again. This time it is—" How had Alresca meant to finish that sentence? "*He* has come again." Who had come again? Was there, then, another man involved in the enigma of this tragedy? Was it the man I had seen opposite the Devonshire Mansion on the night when I had found the dagger? Or was "he" merely an error for "she"? "I love her. *She* has come again." That would surely make better sense than what Alresca had actually written? And he must have been mentally perturbed. Such a slip was possible. No, no! When a man, even a dying man, is writing a message which he has torn out of his heart, he does not put "he" for "she" … "I love her …" Then, had he misjudged her heart when he confided in me during the early part of the evening? Or had the sudden apparition of Rosa created his love anew? Why had she once refused him? She seemed to be sufficiently fond of him. But she had killed him. Directly or indirectly she had been the cause of his death.

And as I looked at her, my profound grief for Alresca made me her judge. I forgot for the instant the feelings with which she had once inspired me, and which, indeed, had never died in my soul.

"How do you explain this?" I demanded of her in a calm and judicial and yet slightly hostile tone.

"Oh!" she exclaimed. "How sad it is! How terribly sad!"

And her voice was so pure and kind, and her glance so innocent, and her grief so pitiful, that I dismissed forever any shade of a suspicion that I might have cherished against her. Although she had avoided my question, although she had ignored its tone, I knew with the certainty of absolute knowledge that she had no more concern in Alresca's death than I had.

She came forward, and regarded the corpse steadily, and took the lifeless hand in her hand. But she did not cry. Then she went abruptly out of the room and out of the house. And for several days I did not see her. A superb wreath arrived with her card, and that was all.

But the positive assurance that she was entirely unconnected with the riddle did nothing to help me to solve it. I had, however, to solve it for the Belgian authorities, and I did so by giving a certificate that Alresca had died of "failure of the heart's action." A convenient phrase, whose convenience imposes perhaps oftener than may be imagined on persons of an unsuspecting turn of mind! And having accounted for Alresca's death to the Belgian authorities, I had no leisure (save during the night) to cogitate much upon the mystery. For I was made immediately to realize, to an extent to which I had not realized before, how great a man Alresca was, and how large he bulked in the world's eye.

The first announcement of his demise appeared in the *Étoile Belgi*, the well-known Brussels daily, and from the moment of its appearance letters, telegrams, and callers descended upon Alresca's house in an unending stream. As his companion I naturally gave the whole of my attention to his affairs, especially as he seemed to have no relatives whatever. Correspondents of English, French, and German newspapers flung themselves upon me in the race for information. They seemed to scent a mystery, but I made it my business to discourage such an idea. Nay, I went further, and deliberately stated to them, with a false air of perfect candour, that there was no foundation of any sort for such an idea. Had not Alresca been indisposed for months? Had he not died from failure of the heart's action? There was no reason why I should have misled these excellent journalists in their search for the sensational truth, except that I preferred to keep the mystery wholly to myself.

Those days after the death recur to me now as a sort of breathless nightmare, in which, aided by the admirable Alexis, I was forever despatching messages and uttering polite phrases to people I had never seen before.

I had two surprises, one greater and one less. In the first place, the Anglo-Belgian lawyer whom I had summoned informed me, after Alresca's papers had been examined and certain effects sealed in the presence of an official, that my friend had made a will, bearing a date immediately before our arrival in Bruges, leaving the whole of his property to me, and appointing me sole executor. I have never understood why Alresca did this, and I have always thought that it was a mere kind caprice on his part.

The second surprise was a visit from the Burgomaster of the city. He came clothed in his official robes. It was a call of the most rigid ceremony. Having condoled with me and also complimented me upon my succession to the dead man's estate, he intimated that the city desired a public funeral. For a moment I was averse to this, but as I could advance no argument against it I concurred in the proposal.

There was a lying-in-state of the body at the cathedral, and the whole city seemed to go in mourning. On the second day a priest called at the house on the Quai des Augustins, and said that he had been sent by the Bishop to ask if I cared to witness the lying-in-state from some private vantage-ground. I went to the cathedral, and the Bishop himself escorted me to the organ-loft, whence I could see the silent crowds move slowly in pairs past Alresca's bier, which lay in the chancel. It was an impressive sight, and one which I shall not forget.

On the afternoon of the day preceding the funeral the same priest came to me again, and I received him in the drawing-room, where I was writing a letter to Totnes. He was an old man, a very old man, with a quavering voice, but he would not sit down.

"It has occurred to the Lord Bishop," he piped, "that monsieur has not been offered the privilege of watching by the bier."

The idea startled me, and I was at a loss what to say.

"The Lord Bishop presents his profound regrets, and will monsieur care to watch?"

I saw at once that a refusal would have horrified the ecclesiastic.

"I shall regard it as an honour," I said. "When?"

"From midnight to two o'clock," answered the priest. "The later watches are arranged."

"It is understood," I said, after a pause.

And the priest departed, charged with my compliments to the Lord Bishop.

I had a horror of the duty which had been thrust upon me. It went against not merely my inclinations but my instincts. However, there was only one thing to do, and of course I did it.

At five minutes to twelve I was knocking at the north door of the cathedral. A sacristan, who carried in his hand a long lighted taper, admitted me at once. Save for this taper and four candles which stood at the four corners of the bier, the vast interior was in darkness.

The sacristan silently pointed to the chancel, and I walked hesitatingly across the gloomy intervening space, my footsteps echoing formidably in the silence. Two young priests stood, one at either side of the lofty bier. One of them bowed to me, and I took his place. He disappeared into the ambulatory. The other priest was praying for the dead, a slight frown on his narrow white brow. His back was half-turned towards the corpse, and he did not seem to notice me in any way.

I folded my arms, and as some relief from the uncanny and troublous thoughts which ran in my head I looked about me. I could not bring myself to gaze on the purple cloth which covered the remains of Alresca. We were alone—the priest, Alresca, and I—and I felt afraid. In vain I glanced round, in order to reassure myself, at the stained-glass windows, now illumined by September starlight, at the beautiful carving of the choir-stalls, at the ugly rococo screen. I was afraid, and there was no disguising my fear.

Suddenly the clock chimes of the belfry rang forth with startling resonance, and twelve o'clock struck upon the stillness. Then followed upon the bells a solemn and funereal melody.

"How comes that?" I asked the priest, without stopping to consider whether I had the right to speak during my vigil.

"It is the carilloneur," my fellow watcher said, interrupting his whispered and sibilant devotions, and turning to me, as it seemed, unwillingly. "Have you not heard it before? Every evening since the death he has played it at midnight in memory of Alresca." Then he resumed his office.

The minutes passed, or rather crawled by, and, if anything, my uneasiness increased. I suffered all the anxieties and tremors which those suffer who pass wakeful nights, imagining every conceivable ill, and victimized by the most dreadful forebodings. Through it all I was conscious of the cold of the stone floor penetrating my boots and chilling my feet ...

The third quarter after one struck, and I began to congratulate myself that the ordeal by the bier was coming to an end. I looked with a sort of bravado into the dark, shadowed distances of the fane, and smiled at my nameless trepidations. And then, as my glance sought to penetrate the gloom of the great western porch, I grew aware that a man stood there. I wished to call the attention of the priest to this man, but I could not—I could not.

He came very quietly out of the porch, and walked with hushed footfall up the nave; he mounted the five steps to the chancel; he approached us; he stood at the foot of the bier; he was within a yard of me. The priest had his back to him. The man seemed to ignore me; he looked fixedly at the bier. But I knew him. I knew that fine, hard, haughty face, that stiff bearing, that implacable eye. It was the man whom I had seen standing under the trees opposite the Devonshire Mansion in London.

For a few moments his countenance showed no emotion. Then the features broke into an expression of indescribable malice. With gestures of demoniac triumph he mocked the solemnity of the bier, and showered upon it every scornful indignity that the human face can convey.

I admit that I was spellbound with astonishment and horror. I ought to have seized the author of the infamous sacrilege—I ought, at any rate, to have called to the priest—but I could do neither. I trembled before this mysterious man. My frame literally shook. I knew what fear was. I was a coward.

At length he turned away, casting at me as he did so one indefinable look, and with slow dignity passed again down the length of the nave and disappeared. Then, and not till then, I found my voice and my courage. I pulled the priest by the sleeve of his cassock.

"Someone has just been in the cathedral," I said huskily. And I told him what I had seen.

"Impossible! *Retro me, Sathanas!* It was imagination."

His tone was dry, harsh.

"No, no," I said eagerly. "I assure you—"

He smiled incredulously, and repeated the word 'Imagination!'

But I well knew that it was not imagination, that I had actually seen this man enter and go forth.

VIII

THE MESSAGE

W HEN I RETURNED TO ALRESCA'S house—or rather, I should say, to my own house—after the moving and picturesque ceremony of the funeral, I found a note from Rosetta Rosa, asking me to call on her at the Hôtel du Commerce. This was the first news of her that I had had since she so abruptly quitted the scene of Alresca's death. I set off instantly for the hotel, and just as I was going I met my Anglo-Belgian lawyer, who presented to me a large envelope addressed to myself in the handwriting of Alresca, and marked 'private.' The lawyer, who had been engaged in the sorting and examination of an enormous quantity of miscellaneous papers left by Alresca, informed me that he only discovered the package that very afternoon. I took the packet, put it in my pocket, and continued on my way to Rosa. It did not occur to me at the time, but it occurred to me afterwards, that I was extremely anxious to see her again.

Everyone who has been to Bruges knows the Hôtel du Commerce. It is the Ritz of Bruges, and very well aware of its own importance in the scheme of things. As I entered the courtyard a waiter came up to me.

"Excuse me, monsieur, but we have no rooms."

"Why do you tell me that?"

"Pardon. I thought monsieur wanted a room. Mademoiselle Rosa, the great diva, is staying here, and all the English from the Hôtel du

Panier d'Or have left there in order to be in the same hotel with Mademoiselle Rosa."

Somewhere behind that mask of professional servility there was a smile.

"I do not want a room," I said, "but I want to see Mademoiselle Rosa."

"Ah! As to that, monsieur, I will inquire." He became stony at once. "Stay. Take my card."

He accepted it, but with an air which implied that everyone left a card.

In a moment another servant came forth, breathing apologies, and led me to Rosa's private sitting-room. As I went in a youngish, dark-eyed, black-aproned woman, who, I had no doubt, was Rosa's maid, left the room.

Rosa and I shook hands in silence, and with a little diffidence. Wrapped in a soft, black, thin-textured tea-gown, she reclined in an easy-chair. Her beautiful face was a dead white; her eyes were dilated, and under them were dark semicircles.

"You have been ill," I exclaimed, "and I was not told."

She shrugged her shoulders in denial, and shivered.

"No," she said shortly. There was a pause. "He is buried?"

"Yes."

"Let me hear about it."

I wished to question her further about her health, but her tone was almost imperious, and I had a curious fear of offending her. Nevertheless I reminded myself that I was a doctor, and my concern for her urged me to be persistent.

"But surely you have been ill?" I said.

She tapped her foot. It was the first symptom of nervous impatience that I had observed in her.

"Not in body," she replied curtly. "Tell me all about the funeral."

And I gave her an account of the impressive incidents of the interment—the stately procession, the grandiose ritual, the symbols of public grief. She displayed a strange, morbid curiosity as to it all.

And then suddenly she rose up from her chair, and I rose also, and she demanded, as it were pushed by some secret force to the limit of her endurance:

"You loved him, didn't you, Mr Foster?"

It was not an English phrase; no Englishwoman would have used it.

"I was tremendously fond of him," I answered. "I should never have thought that I could have grown so fond of anyone in such a short time. He wasn't merely fine as an artist; he was so fine as a man."

She nodded.

"You understood him? You knew all about him? He talked to you openly, didn't he?"

"Yes," I said. "He used to tell me all kinds of things."

"Then explain to me," she cried out, and I saw that tears brimmed in her eyes, "why did he die when I came?"

"It was a coincidence," I said lamely.

Seizing my hands, she actually fell on her knees before me, flashing into my eyes all the loveliness of her pallid, upturned face.

"It was not a coincidence!" she passionately sobbed. "Why can't you be frank with me, and tell me how it is that I have killed him? He said long ago—do you not remember?—that I was fatal to him. He was getting better—you yourself said so—till I came, and then he died."

What could I reply? The girl was uttering the thoughts which had haunted me for days.

I tried to smile a reassurance, and raising her as gently as I could, I led her back to her chair. It was on my part a feeble performance.

"You are suffering from a nervous crisis," I said, "and I must prescribe for you. My first prescription is that we do not talk about Alresca's death."

I endeavoured to be perfectly matter-of-fact in tone, and gradually she grew calmer.

"I have not slept since that night," she murmured wearily. "Then you will not tell me?"

"What have I to tell you, except that you are ill? Stop a moment. I have an item of news, after all. Poor Alresca has made me his heir."

"That was like his kind heart."

"Yes, indeed. But I can't imagine why he did it!"

"It was just gratitude," said she.

"A rare kind of gratitude," I replied.

"Is no reason given in the will?"

"Not a word."

I remembered the packet which I had just received from the lawyer, and I mentioned it to her.

"Open it now," she said. "I am interested—if you do not think me too inquisitive."

I tore the envelope. It contained another envelope, sealed, and a letter. I scanned the letter.

"It is nothing," I said with false casualness, and was returning it to my pocket. The worst of me is that I have no histrionic instinct; I cannot act a part.

"Wait!" she cried sharply, and I hesitated before the appeal in her tragic voice. "You cannot deceive me, Mr Foster. It *is* something. I entreat you to read to me that letter. Does it not occur to you that I have the right to demand this from you? Why should he beat about the bush? You know, and I know that you know, that there is a mystery in this dreadful death. Be frank with me, my friend. I have suffered much these last days."

We looked at each other silently, I with the letter in my hand. Why, indeed, should I treat her as a child, this woman with the compelling eyes, the firm, commanding forehead? Why should I pursue the silly game of pretence?

"I will read it," I said. "There is, certainly, a mystery in connection with Alresca's death, and we may be on the eve of solving it."

The letter was dated concurrently with Alresca's will—that is to say, a few days before our arrival in Bruges—and it ran thus:

My dear Friend,

It seems to me that I am to die, and from a strange cause—for I believe I have guessed the cause. The nature of my guess and all the circumstances I have written out at length, and the document is in the sealed packet which accompanies this. My reason for making such a record is a peculiar one. I should desire that no eye might ever read that document. But I have an idea that some time or other the record may be of use to you—possibly soon. You, Carl, may be the heir of more than my goods. If matters should so fall out, then break the seal, and read what I have written. If not, I beg of you, after five years have elapsed, to destroy the packet unread. I do not care to be more precise.

Always yours,

Alresca

"That is all?" asked Rosa, when I had finished reading it.

I passed her the letter to read for herself. Her hand shook as she returned it to me.

And we both blushed. We were both confused, and each avoided the glance of the other. The silence between us was difficult to bear. I broke it.

"The question is, What am I to do? Alresca is dead. Shall I respect his wish, or shall I open the packet now? If he could have foreseen your anxiety, he probably would not have made these conditions. Besides, who can say that the circumstances he hints at have not already arisen? Who can say"—I uttered the words with an emphasis the daring of which astounded even myself—"that I am not already the heir of more than Alresca's goods?"

I imagined, after achieving this piece of audacity, that I was perfectly calm, but within me there must have raged such a tumult of love and dark foreboding that in reality I could scarcely have known what I was about.

Rosa's eyes fixed themselves upon me, but I sustained that gaze. She stretched forth a hand as if to take the packet.

"You shall decide," I said. "Am I to open it, or am I not to open it?"

"Open it," she whispered. "He will forgive us."

I began to break the seal.

"No, no!" she screamed, standing up again with clenched hands. "I was wrong. Leave it, for God's sake! I could not bear to know the truth."

I, too, sprang up, electrified by that terrible outburst. Grasping tight the envelope, I walked to and fro in the room, stamping on the carpet, and wondering all the time (in one part of my brain) why I should be making such a noise with my feet. At length I faced her. She had not moved. She stood like a statue, her black tea-gown falling about her, and her two hands under her white drawn face.

"It shall be as you wish," I said. "I won't open it."

And I put the envelope back into my pocket.

We both sat down.

"Let us have some tea, eh?" said Rosa. She had resumed her self-control more quickly than I could. I was unable to answer her matter-of-fact remark. She rang the bell, and the maid entered with tea. The girl's features struck me; they showed both wit and cunning.

"What splendid tea!" I said, when the refection was in progress. We had both found it convenient to shelter our feelings behind small talk. "I'd no idea you could get tea like this in Bruges."

"You can't," Rosa smiled. "I never travel without my own brand. It is one of Yvette's special cares not to forget it."

"Your maid?"

"Yes."

"She seems not quite the ordinary maid," I ventured.

"Yvette? No! I should think not. She has served half the sopranos in Europe—she won't go to contraltos. I possess her because I outbid all rivals for her services. As a hairdresser she is unequalled. And it's so much nicer not being forced to call in a coiffeur in every town! It was she who invented my 'Elsa' coiffure. Perhaps you remember it?"

"Perfectly. By the way, when do you recommence your engagements?"

She smiled nervously. "I—I haven't decided."

Nothing with any particle of significance passed during the remainder of our interview. Telling her that I was leaving for England the next day, I bade good-by to Rosa. She did not express the hope of seeing me again, and for some obscure reason, buried in the mysteries of love's psychology, I dared not express the hope to her. And so we parted, with a thousand things unsaid, on a note of ineffectuality, of suspense, of vague indefiniteness.

And the next morning I received from her this brief missive, which threw me into a wild condition of joyous expectancy:

> If you could meet me in the Church of St Gilles at eleven o'clock this morning, I should like to have your advice upon a certain matter.—Rosa.

Seventy-seven years elapsed before eleven o'clock.

St Gilles is a large church in a small deserted square at the back of the town. I waited for Rosa in the western porch, and at five minutes past the hour she arrived, looking better in health, at once more composed and vivacious. We sat down in a corner at the far end of one of the aisles. Except ourselves and a couple of cleaners, there seemed to be no one in the church.

"You asked me yesterday about my engagements," she began.

"Yes," I said, "and I had a reason. As a doctor, I will take leave to tell you that it is advisable for you to throw yourself into your work as soon as possible, and as completely as possible." And I remembered the similar advice which, out of the plenitude of my youthful wisdom, I had offered to Alresca only a few days before.

"The fact is that I have signed a contract to sing *Carmen* at the Paris Opéra Comique in a fortnight's time. I have never sung the role there before, and I am, or rather I was, very anxious to do so. This morning I had a telegram from the manager urging me to go to Paris without delay for the rehearsals."

"And are you going?"

"That is the question. I may tell you that one of my objects in calling on poor Alresca was to consult him about the point. The truth is, I am threatened with trouble if I appear at the Opéra Comique, particularly in *Carmen*. The whole matter is paltry beyond words, but really I am a little afraid."

"May I hear the story?"

"You know Carlotta Deschamps, who always takes *Carmen* at the Comique?"

"I've heard her sing."

"By the way, that is her half-sister, Marie Deschamps, who sings in your cousin's operas at the London Diana."

"I have made the acquaintance of Marie—a harmless little thing!"

"Her half-sister isn't quite so harmless. She is the daughter of a Spanish mother, while Marie is the daughter of an English mother, a Cockney woman. As to Carlotta, when I was younger"—oh, the deliciously aged air with which this creature of twenty-three referred to her youth—"I was singing at the Opéra Comique in Paris, where Carlotta was starring, and I had the misfortune to arouse her jealousy. She is frightfully jealous, and gets worse as she gets older. She swore to me that if I ever dared to appear at the Comique again she would have me killed. I laughed. I forgot the affair, but it happens that I never have sung at the Comique since that time. And now that I am not merely to appear at the Comique, but am going to sing *Carmen* there, her own particular role, Deschamps is furious. I firmly believe she means harm. Twice she has written to me the most formidable threats. It seems strange that I should stand in awe of a woman like Carlotta Deschamps, but so it is. I am half-inclined to throw up the engagement."

That a girl of Rosa's spirit should have hesitated for an instant about fulfilling her engagement showed most plainly, I thought, that she was not herself. I assured her that her fears were groundless, that we lived in the nineteenth century, and that Deschamps' fury would spend itself in nothing worse than threats. In the end she said she would reconsider the matter.

"Don't wait to reconsider," I urged, "but set off for Paris at once. Go to-day. Act. It will do you good."

"But there are a hundred things to be thought of first," she said, laughing at my earnestness.

"For example?"

"Well, my jewels are with my London bankers."

"Can't you sing without jewels?"

"Not in Paris. Who ever heard of such a thing?"

"You can write to your bankers to send them by registered post."

"Post! They are worth thousands and thousands of pounds. I ought really to fetch them, but there would scarcely be time."

"Let me bring them to you in Paris," I said. "Give me a letter to your bankers, and I will undertake to deliver the jewels safely into your hands."

"I could not dream of putting you to so much trouble."

The notion of doing something for her had, however, laid hold of me. At that moment I felt that to serve even as her jewel-carrier would be for me the supreme happiness in the world.

"But," I said, "I ask it as a favour."

"Do you?" She gave me a divine smile, and yielded.

At her request we did not leave the church together. She preceded me. I waited a few minutes, and then walked slowly out. Happening to look back as I passed along the square, I saw a woman's figure which was familiar to me, and, dominated by a sudden impulse, I returned quickly on my steps. The woman was Yvette, and she was obviously a little startled when I approached her.

"Are you waiting for your mistress?" I said sharply. "Because …"

She flashed me a look.

"Did monsieur by any chance imagine that I was waiting for himself?"

There was a calm insolence about the girl which induced me to retire from that parley.

In two hours I was on my way to London.

IX

THE TRAIN

THE BOAT-TRAIN WAS DUE TO leave in ten minutes, and the platform at Victoria Station (how changed since then!) showed that scene of discreet and haughty excitement which it was wont to exhibit about nine o'clock every evening in those days. The weather was wild. It had been wet all day, and the rain came smashing down, driven by the great gusts of a genuine westerly gale. Consequently there were fewer passengers than usual, and those people who by choice or compulsion had resolved to front the terrors of the Channel passage had a preoccupied look as they hurried importantly to and fro amid piles of luggage and groups of loungers on the wind-swept platform beneath the flickering gas-lamps. But the porters, and the friends engaged in the ceremony of seeing-off, and the loungers, and the bookstall clerks—these individuals were not preoccupied by thoughts of intimate inconveniences before midnight. As for me, I was quite alone with my thoughts. At least, I began by being alone.

As I was registering a particularly heavy and overfed portmanteau to Paris, a young woman put her head close to mine at the window of the baggage-office.

"Mr Foster? I thought it was. My cab set down immediately after yours, and I have been trying to catch your eye on the platform. Of course it was no go!"

The speech was thrown at me in a light, airy tone from a tiny, pert mouth which glistened red behind a muslin veil.

"Miss Deschamps!" I exclaimed.

"Glad you remember my name. As handsome and supercilious as ever, I observe. I haven't seen you since that night at Sullivan's reception. Why didn't you call on me one Sunday? You know I asked you to."

"Did you ask me?" I demanded, secretly flattered in the extremity of my youthfulness because she had called me supercilious.

"Well, rather. I'm going to Paris—and in this weather!"

"I am, too."

"Then, let's go together, eh?"

"Delighted. But why have you chosen such a night?"

"I haven't chosen it. You see, I open to-morrow at the Casino de Paris for fourteen nights, and I suppose I've got to be there. You wouldn't believe what they're paying me. The Diana company is touring in the provinces while the theatre is getting itself decorated. I hate the provinces. Leeds and Liverpool and Glasgow—fancy dancing there! And so my half-sister—Carlotta, y'know—got me this engagement, and I'm going to stay with her. Have you met Carlotta?"

"No—not yet." I did not add that I had had reason to think a good deal about her.

"Well, Carlotta is—Carlotta. A terrific swell, and a bit of a Tartar. We quarrel every time we meet, which isn't often. She tries to play the elder sister game on me, and I won't have it. Though she is elder—very much elder, you now. But I think her worst point is that she's so frightfully mysterious. You can never tell what she's up to. Now, a man I met at supper last night told me he thought he had seen Carlotta in Bloomsbury yesterday. However, I didn't believe that, because she is expecting me in Paris; we happen to be as thick as thieves just now, and if she had been in London, she would have looked me up."

"Just so," I replied, wondering whether I should endeavour to obtain from Marie Deschamps information which would be useful to Rosa.

By the time that the star of the Diana had said goodbye to certain male acquaintances, and had gone through a complicated dialogue with her maid on the subject of dress-trunks, the clock pointed almost to nine, and a porter rushed us—Marie and myself—into an empty compartment of a composite coach near to the engine. The compartment was first class, but it evidently belonged to an ancient order of rolling stock, and the vivacious Marie criticized it with considerable freedom. The wind howled, positively howled, in the station.

"I wish I wasn't going," said the lady. "I shall be horribly ill."

"You probably will," I said, to tease her, idly opening the *Globe*. "It seems that the morning steamer from Calais wasn't able to make either Dover or Folkestone, and has returned to Calais. Imagine the state of mind of the passengers!"

"Ugh! Oh, Mr Foster, what *is* that case by your side?"

"It is a jewel-case."

"What a big one!"

She did not conceal her desire to see the inside of it, but I felt that I could not, even to satisfy her charming curiosity, expose the interior of Rosa's jewel-case in a railway carriage, and so I edged away from the topic with as much adroitness as I was capable of.

The pretty girl pouted, and asked me for the *Globe*, behind which she buried herself. She kept murmuring aloud extracts from the *Globe's* realistic description of the weather, and then she jumped up.

"I'm not going."

"Not going?"

"No. The weather's too awful. These newspaper accounts frighten me."

"But the Casino de Paris?"

"A fig for it! They must wait for me, that's all. I'll try again to-morrow. Will you mind telling the guard to get my boxes out, there's a dear Mr Foster, and I'll endeavour to find that maid of mine?"

The train was already five minutes late in starting; she delayed it quite another five minutes, and enjoyed the process. And it was I who meekly received the objurgations of porters and guard. My reward was a smile, given with a full sense of its immense value.

"Good-bye, Mr Foster. Take care of your precious jewel-case."

I had carried the thing in my hand up and down the platform. I ran to my carriage, and jumped in breathless as the train whistled.

"Pleasant journey!" the witch called out, waving her small hand to me.

I bowed to her from the window, laughing. She was a genial soul, and the incident had not been without amusement.

After I had shut the carriage door, and glanced out of the window for a moment in the approved way, I sank, faintly smiling at the episode, into my corner, and then I observed with a start that the opposite corner was occupied. Another traveller had got into the compartment while I had been coursing about the platform on behalf of Marie, and that traveller was the mysterious and sinister creature whom I had met twice before—once in Oxford Street, and once again during the night watch in the cathedral at Bruges. He must have made up his mind to travel rather suddenly, for, in spite of the weather, he had neither overcoat nor umbrella—merely the frock coat and silk hat of Piccadilly. But there was no spot of rain on him, and no sign of disarray.

As I gazed with alarmed eyes into the face of that strange, forbidding personality, the gaiety of my mood went out like a match in a breeze. The uncomfortable idea oppressed me that I was being surely caught and enveloped in a net of adverse circumstances, that I was the unconscious victim of a deep and terrible conspiracy which proceeded slowly forward to an inevitable catastrophe. On each of the previous occasions when this silent and malicious man had crossed my path I had had the same feeling, but in a less degree, and I had been able to shake it off almost at once. But now it overcame and conquered me.

The train thundered across Grosvenor Bridge through the murky weather on its way to the coast, and a hundred times I cursed it for its lack of speed. I would have given much to be at the journey's end, and away from this motionless and inscrutable companion. His eyes were constantly on my face, and do what I would I could not appear at ease. I tried to read the paper, I pretended to sleep, I hummed a tune, I even went so far as to whistle, but my efforts at sang-froid were ridiculous. The worst of it was that he was aware of my despicable condition; his changeless cynical smile made that fact obvious to me.

At last I felt that something must happen. At any rate, the silence of the man must be broken. And so I gathered together my courage, and with a preposterous attempt at a friendly smile remarked:

"Beastly weather we're having. One would scarcely expect it so early in September."

It was an inane speech, so commonplace, so entirely foolish. And the man ignored it absolutely. Only the corners of his lips drooped a little to express, perhaps, a profounder degree of hate and scorn.

This made me a little angry.

"Didn't I see you last in the cathedral at Bruges?" I demanded curtly, even rudely.

He laughed. And his laugh really alarmed me.

The train stopped at that moment at a dark and deserted spot, which proved to be Sittingbourne. I hesitated, and then, giving up the struggle, sped out of the compartment, and entered another one lower down. My new compartment was empty. The sensation of relief was infinitely soothing. Placing the jewel-case carefully on my knees, I breathed freely once more, and said to myself that another quarter of an hour of that detestable presence would have driven me mad.

I began to think about Rosetta Rosa. As a solace after the exasperating companionship of that silent person in the other compartment, I invited from the back of my mind certain thoughts about Rosetta Rosa which had been modestly waiting for me there for some little time, and I looked at them fairly, and turned them over, and viewed them from every side, and derived from them a rather thrilling joy. The fact is, I was beginning to be in love with Rosa. Nay, I was actually in love with her. Ever since our first meeting my meditations had been more or less busy with her image. For a long period, largely owing to my preoccupation with Alresca, I had dreamed of her but vaguely. And now, during our interviews at her hotel and in the church of St Gilles, she had, in the most innocent way in the world, forged fetters on me which I had no desire to shake off.

It was a presumption on my part. I acknowledged frankly that it was a presumption. I was a young doctor, with nothing to distinguish me from the ruck of young doctors. And she was—well, she was one of those rare and radiant beings to whom even monarchs bow, and the whole earth offers the incense of its homage.

Which did not in the least alter the fact that I was in love with her. And, after all, she was just a woman; more, she was a young woman. And she had consulted me! She had allowed me to be of use to her! And, months ago in London, had she not permitted me to talk to her with an extraordinary freedom? Lovely, incomparable, exquisite as she was, she was nevertheless a girl, and I was sure that she had a girl's heart.

However, it was a presumption.

I remembered her legendary engagement to Lord Clarenceux, an engagement which had interested all Europe. I often thought of that matter. Had she loved him—really loved him? Or had his love for her merely flattered her into thinking that she loved him? Would she not be liable to institute comparisons between myself and that renowned, wealthy, and gifted nobleman?

Well, I did not care if she did. Such is the egoism of untried love that I did not care if she did! And I lapsed into a reverie—a reverie in which everything went smoothly, everything was for the best in the best of all possible worlds, and only love and love's requital existed …

Then, in the fraction of a second, as it seemed, there was a grating, a horrible grind of iron, a bump, a check, and my head was buried in the cushions of the opposite side of the carriage, and I felt stunned—not much, but a little.

"What—what?" I heard myself exclaim. "They must have plumped the brakes on pretty sudden."

Then, quite after an interval, it occurred to me that this was a railway accident—one of those things that one reads of in the papers with so much calmness. I wondered if I was hurt, and why I could hear no sound; the silence was absolute—terrifying.

In a vague, aimless way, I sought for my matchbox, and struck a light. I had just time to observe that both windows were smashed, and the floor of the compartment tilted, when the match went out in the wind. I had heard no noise of breaking glass.

I stumbled slowly to the door, and tried to open it, but the thing would not budge. Whereupon I lost my temper.

"Open, you beast, you beast, you beast!" I cried to the door, kicking it hard, and yet not feeling the impact.

Then another thought—a proud one, which served to tranquillize me: "I am a doctor, and they will want me to attend to the wounded."

I remembered my flask, and unscrewing the stopper with difficulty, clutched the mouth with my teeth and drank. After that I was sane and collected. Now I could hear people tramping on the ground outside, and see the flash of lanterns. In another moment a porter, whose silver buttons gleamed in the darkness, was pulling me through the window.

"Hurt?"

"No, not I. But if anyone else is, I'm a doctor."

"Here's a doctor, sir," he yelled to a grey-headed man near by. Then he stood still, wondering what he should do next. I perceived in the near distance the lights of a station.

"Is that Dover?"

"No, sir; Dover Priory. Dover's a mile further on. There was a goods wagon got derailed on the siding just beyond the home signal, and it blocked the down line, and the driver of the express ran right into it, although the signal was against him—ran right into it, 'e did."

Other people were crawling out of the carriages now, and suddenly there seemed to be scores of spectators, and much shouting and running about. The engine lay on its side, partly overhanging a wrecked wagon. Immense clouds of steam issued from it, hissing above the roar of the wind. The tender was twisted like a patent hairpin in the middle. The first coach, a luggage-van, stood upright, and seemed scarcely damaged. The second coach, the small, old-fashioned vehicle which happily I had abandoned at Sittingbourne, was smashed out of resemblance to a coach. The third one, from which I had just emerged, looked fairly healthy, and the remaining three had not even left the rails.

All ran to the smashed coach.

"There were two passengers in that coach," said the guard, who, having been at the rear of the train, was unharmed.

"Are you counting me?" I asked. "Because I changed carriages at Sittingbourne."

"Praise God for that, sir!" he answered. "There's only one, then—a tall, severe-looking gent—in the first-class compartment."

Was it joy or sorrow that I felt at the thought of that man buried somewhere in the shapeless mass of wood and iron? It certainly was not unmixed sorrow. On the contrary, I had a distinct feeling of elation at the thought that I was probably rid forever of this haunter of my peace, this menacing and mysterious existence which (if instinctive foreboding was to be trusted) had been about to cross and thwart and blast my own.

The men hammered and heaved and chopped and sawed, and while they were in the midst of the work someone took me by the sleeve and asked me to go and attend to the engine-driver and stoker, who were being carried into a waiting-room at the station. It is symptomatic of the extraordinary confusion which reigns in these affairs that till that moment the question of the fate of the men in charge of the train had not even entered my mind, though I had of course noticed that the engine was overturned. In the waiting-room it was discovered that two local doctors had already arrived. I preferred to leave the engine-driver to them. He was unconscious as he lay on a table. The stoker, by his side, kept murmuring in a sort of delirium:

"Bill, 'e was all dazed like—'e was all dazed like. I told him the signal wasn't off. I shouted to him. But 'e was all dazed like."

I returned to the train full of a horrible desire to see with my own eyes a certain corpse. Bit by bit the breakdown gang had removed the whole of the centre part of the shattered carriage. I thrust myself into the group, and—we all looked at each other. Nobody, alive or dead, was to be found.

"He, too, must have got out at Sittingbourne," I said at length.

"Ay!" said the guard.

My heard swam, dizzy with dark imaginings and unspeakable suspicions. "He has escaped; he is alive!" I muttered savagely, hopelessly. It was as if a doom had closed inevitably over me. But if my thoughts had been legible and I had been asked to explain this attitude of mine towards a person who had never spoken to me, whom I had seen but thrice, and whose identity was utterly unknown, I could not have done so. I had no reasons. It was intuition.

Abruptly I straightened myself, and surveying the men and the background of ruin lighted by the fitful gleams of lanterns and the pale glitter of a moon half-hidden by flying clouds, I shouted out:

"I want a cab. I have to catch the Calais boat. Will somebody please direct me!"

No one appeared even to hear me. The mental phenomena which accompany a railway accident, even a minor one such as this, are of the most singular description. I felt that I was growing angry again. I had a grievance because not a soul there seemed to care whether I caught the Calais boat or not. That, under the unusual circumstances, the steamer would probably wait did not occur to me. Nor did I perceive that there was no real necessity for me to catch the steamer. I might just as well have spent the night at the Lord Warden, and proceeded on my journey in the morning. But no! I must hurry away instantly!

Then I thought of the jewel-box.

"Where's my jewel-box?" I demanded vehemently from the guard, as though he had stolen it.

He turned to me.

"What's that you're carrying?" he replied.

All the time I had been carrying the jewel-box. At the moment of the collision I must have instinctively clutched it, and my grasp had not slackened. I had carried it to the waiting-room and back without knowing that I was doing so!

This sobered me once more. But I would not stay on the scene. I was still obsessed by the desire to catch the steamer. And abruptly I set off walking down the line. I left the crowd and the confusion and the ruin, and hastened away bearing the box.

I think that I must have had no notion of time, and very little notion of space. For I arrived at the harbour without the least recollection of the details of my journey thither. I had no memory of having been accosted by any official of the railway, or even of having encountered any person at all. Fortunately it had ceased to rain, and the wind, though still strong, was falling rapidly.

Except for a gatekeeper, the bleak, exposed pier had the air of being deserted. The lights of the town flickered in the distance, and above them rose dimly the gaunt outlines of the fortified hills. In front was the intemperate and restless sea. I felt that I was at the extremity of England, and on the verge of unguessed things. Now, I had traversed about half the length of the lonely pier, which seems to curve right out into the unknown, when I saw a woman approaching me in the opposite direction. My faculties were fatigued with the crowded sensations of that evening, and I took no notice of her. Even when she stopped to peer into my face I thought nothing of it, and put her gently aside, supposing her to be some dubious character of the night hours. But she insisted on speaking to me.

"You are Carl Foster," she said abruptly. The voice was harsh, trembling, excited, yet distinguished.

"Suppose I am?" I answered wearily. How tired I was!

"I advise you not to go to Paris."

I began to arouse my wits, and I became aware that the woman was speaking with a strong French accent. I searched her face, but she wore a thick veil, and in the gloom of the pier I could only make out that she had striking features, and was probably some forty years of age. I stared at her in silence.

"I advise you not to go to Paris," she repeated.

"Who are you?"

"Never mind. Take my advice."

"Why? Shall I be robbed?"

"Robbed!" she exclaimed, as if that was a new idea to her. "Yes," she said hurriedly. "Those jewels might be stolen."

"How do you know that I have jewels?"

"Ah! I—I saw the case."

"Don't trouble yourself, madam; I shall take particular care not to be robbed. But may I ask how you have got hold of my name?"

I had vague ideas of an ingenious plan for robbing me, the particulars of which this woman was ready to reveal for a consideration.

She ignored my question.

"Listen!" she said quickly. "You are going to meet a lady in Paris. Is it not so?"

"I must really—"

"Take advice. Move no further in that affair."

I attempted to pass her, but she held me by the sleeve. She went on with emphasis:

"Rosetta Rosa will never be allowed to sing in *Carmen* at the Opéra Comique. Do you understand?"

"Great Scott!" I said, "I believe you must be Carlotta Deschamps."

It was a half-humorous inspiration on my part, but the remark produced an immediate effect on the woman, for she walked away with a highly theatrical scowl and toss of the head. I recalled what Marie Deschamps had said in the train about her stepsister, and also my suspicion that Rosa's maid was not entirely faithful to her mistress—spied on her, in fact; and putting the two things together, it occurred to me that this strange lady might actually be Carlotta.

Many women of the stage acquire a habitual staginess and theatricality, and it was quite conceivable that Carlotta had relations with Yvette, and that, ridden by the old jealousy which had been aroused through the announcement of Rosa's return to the Opéra Comique, she was setting herself in an indefinite, clumsy, stealthy, and melodramatic manner to prevent Rosa's appearance in *Carmen*.

No doubt she had been informed of Rosa's conference with me in the church of St Gilles, and, impelled by some vague, obscure motive, had travelled to London to discover me, and having succeeded, was determined by some means to prevent me from getting into touch with Rosa in Paris. So I conjectured roughly, and subsequent events indicated that I was not too far wrong.

I laughed. The notion of the middle-aged *prima donna* going about in waste places at dead of night to work mischief against a rival was indubitably comic. I would make a facetious narrative of the meeting for the amusement of Rosa at breakfast to-morrow in Paris. Then, feeling all at once at the end of my physical powers, I continued my way, and descended the steps to the Calais boat.

All was excitement there. Had I heard of the railway accident? Yes, I had. I had been in it. Instantly I was surrounded by individuals who raked me fore and aft with questions. I could not endure it; my nervous energy, I realized, was exhausted, and having given a brief outline of the disaster, I fled down the saloon stairs.

My sole desire was to rest; the need of unconsciousness, of forgetfulness, was imperious upon me; I had had too many experiences during the last few hours. I stretched myself on the saloon cushions, making a pillow of the jewel-box.

"Shall we start soon?" I murmured to a steward.

"Yes, sir, in another five minutes. Weather's moderating, sir."

Other passengers were in the saloon, and more followed. As this would be the first steamer to leave Dover that day, there was a good number of voyagers on board, in spite of adverse conditions. I heard people talking, and the splash of waves against the vessel's sides, and then I went to sleep. Nothing could have kept me awake.

X

THE STEAMER

I AWOKE WITH A START, and with wavering eyes looked at the saloon clock. I had slept for one hour only, but it appeared to me that I was quite refreshed. My mind was strangely clear, every sense preternaturally alert. I began to wonder what had aroused me. Suddenly the ship shuddered through the very heart of her, and I knew that it was this shuddering, which must have occurred before, that had wakened me.

"Good God! We're sinking!" a man cried. He was in the next berth to me, and he sat up, staring wildly.

"Rubbish!" I answered.

The electric lights went out, and we were left with the miserable illumination of one little swinging oil-lamp. Immediately the score or so persons in the saloon were afoot and rushing about, grasping their goods and chattels. The awful shuddering of the ship continued. Scarcely a word was spoken.

A man flew, or rather, tumbled, down the saloon stairs, shouting: "Where's my wife? Where's my wife?" No one took the slightest notice of him, nor did he seem to expect any answer. Even in the semi-darkness of the single lamp I distinctly saw that with both hands he was tearing handfuls of hair from his head. I had heard the phrase "tearing one's hair" some thousands of times in my life, but never till that moment had I witnessed the action itself. Somehow it made an impression on me. The man raced round the saloon still shouting, and raced away again upstairs and out of sight. Everyone followed him pell-mell, helter-skelter, and almost in a second I found myself alone. I put on my overcoat, and my mackintosh over that, and seizing Rosa's jewel-box, I followed the crowd.

As I emerged on deck a Bengal light flared red and dazzling on the bridge, and I saw some sailors trying to lower a boat from its davits. Then I knew that the man who had cried "We're sinking!" even if he was not speaking the exact truth, had at any rate some grounds for his assertion.

A rather pretty girl, pale with agitation, seized me by the buttonhole.

"Where are we going?" she questioned earnestly.

"Don't know, madam," I replied; and then a young man dragged her off by the arm.

"Come this way, Lottie," I heard him say to her, "and keep calm."

I was left staring at the place where the girl's head had been. Then the head of an old man filled that place. I saw his mouth and all his features working in frantic endeavour to speak to me, but he could not articulate. I stepped aside; I could not bear to look at him.

"Carl," I said to myself, "you are undoubtedly somewhat alarmed, but you are not in such an absolutely azure funk as that old chap. Pull yourself together."

Of what followed immediately I have no recollection. I knew vaguely that the ship rolled and had a serious list to starboard, that orders were being hoarsely shouted from the bridge, that the moon was shining fitfully, that the sea was black and choppy; I also seemed to catch the singing of a hymn somewhere on the forward deck. I suppose I knew that I existed. But that was all. I had no exact knowledge of what I myself was doing. There was a hiatus in my consciousness of myself.

The proof of this is that, after a lapse of time, I suddenly discovered that I had smoked half-way through a cigarette, and that I was at the bows of the steamer. For a million sovereigns I could not explain under what circumstances I had moved from one end of the ship to the other, nor how I had come to light that cigarette. Such is the curious effect of perturbation.

But the perturbation had now passed from me, just as mysteriously as it had overtaken me. I was cool and calm. I felt inquisitive, and I asked several people what had happened. But none seemed to know. In fact, they scarcely heard me, and answered wildly, as if in delirium. It seemed strange that anything could have occurred on so small a vessel without the precise details being common property. Yet so it was, and those who have been in an accident at sea will support me when I say that the ignorance on the part of the passengers of the events actually in progress is not the least astounding nor the least disconcerting item in such an affair. It was the psychology of the railway accident repeated.

I began to observe. The weather was a little murky, but beyond doubt still improving. The lights of the French coast could clearly be seen. The ship rolled in a short sea; her engines had stopped; she still had the formidable list to starboard; the captain was on the bridge, leaning over, and with his hands round his mouth was giving orders to an officer below. The sailors were still struggling to lower the boat from the davits. The passengers stood about, aimless, perhaps terror-struck, but now for the most part quiet and self-contained. Some of them had life-belts. That was the sum of my observations.

A rocket streamed upwards into the sky, and another and another, then one caught the rigging, and, deflected, whizzed down again within a few feet of my head, and dropped on deck, spluttering in a silly, futile way. I threw the end of my cigarette at it to see whether that might help it along.

"So this is a shipwreck," I ejaculated. "And I'm in it. I've got myself safely off the railway only to fall into the sea. What a d——d shame!"

Queerly enough, I had ceased to puzzle myself with trying to discover how the disaster had been brought about. I honestly made up my mind that we were sinking, and that was sufficient.

"What cursed ill-luck!" I murmured philosophically.

I thought of Rosa, with whom I was to have breakfasted on the morrow, whose jewels I was carrying, whose behest it had been my pleasure to obey. At that moment she seemed to me in my mind's eye more beautiful, of a more exquisite charm, than ever before. "Am I going to lose her?" I murmured. And then: "What a sensation there'll be in the papers if this ship does go down!" My brain flitted from point to point in a quick agitation. I decided suddenly that the captain and crew must be a set of nincompoops, who had lost their heads, and, not knowing what to do, were unserenely doing nothing. And quite as suddenly I reversed my decision, and reflected that no doubt the captain was doing precisely the correct thing, and that the crew were loyal and disciplined.

Then my mind returned to Rosa. What would she say, what would she feel, when she learnt that I had been drowned in the Channel? Would she experience a grief merely platonic, or had she indeed a profounder feeling towards me? Drowned! Who said drowned? There were the boats, if they could be launched, and, moreover, I could swim. I considered what I should do at the moment the ship foundered—for I still felt she would founder. I was the blackest of pessimists. I said to myself that I would spring as far as I could into the sea, not only to avoid the sucking in of the vessel, but to get clear of the other passengers.

Suppose that a passenger who could not swim should by any chance seize me in the water, how should I act? This was a conundrum. I could not save another and myself, too. I said I would leave that delicate point till the time came, but in my heart I knew that I should beat off such a person with all the savagery of despair—unless it happened to be a woman. I felt that I could not repulse a drowning woman, even if to help her for a few minutes meant death for both of us.

How insignificant seemed everything else—everything outside the ship and the sea and our perilous plight! The death of Alresca, the jealousy of Carlotta Deschamps, the plot (if there was one) against Rosa—what were these matters to me? But Rosa was something. She was more than something; she was all. A lovely, tantalizing vision of her appeared to float before my eyes.

I peered over the port rail to see whether we were in fact gradually sinking. The heaving water looked a long way off, and the idea of this raised my spirits for an instant. But only for an instant. The apparent inactivity of those in charge annoyed while it saddened me. They were not even sending up rockets now, nor burning Bengal lights. I had no patience left to ask more questions. A mood of disgust seized me. If the captain himself had stood by my side waiting to reply to requests for information, I doubt if I should have spoken. I felt like the spectator who is compelled to witness a tragedy which both wounds and bores him. I was obsessed by my own ill-luck and the stupidity of the rest of mankind. I was particularly annoyed by the spasmodic hymn-singing that went on in various parts of the deck.

The man who had burst into the saloon shouting "Where is my wife?" reappeared from somewhere, and standing near to me started to undress hastily. I watched him. He had taken off his coat, waistcoat, and boots, when a quiet, amused voice said: "I shouldn't do that if I were you. It's rather chilly, you know. Besides, think of the ladies."

Without a word he began with equal celerity to reassume his clothes. I turned to the speaker. It was the youth who had dragged the girl away from me when I first came up on deck. She was on his arm, and had a rug over her head. Both were perfectly self-possessed. The serenity of the young man's face particularly struck me. I was not to be out-done.

"Have a cigarette?" I said.

"Thanks."

"Do you happen to know what all this business is?" I asked him.

"It's a collision," he said. "We were struck on the port paddle-box. That saved us for the moment."

"How did it occur?"

"Don't know."

"And where's the ship that struck us?"

"Oh, somewhere over there—two or three miles away." He pointed vaguely to the northeast. "You see, half the paddle-wheel was knocked off, and when that sank, of course the port side rose out of the water. I believe those paddle-wheels weigh a deuce of a lot."

"Are we going to sink?"

"Don't know. Can tell you more in half an hour. I've got two life-belts hidden under a seat. They're rather a nuisance to carry about. You're shivering, Lottie. We must take some more exercise. See you later, sir."

And the two went off again. The girl had not looked at me, nor I at her. She did not seem to be interested in our conversation. As for her companion, he restored my pride in my race.

I began to whistle. Suddenly the whistle died on my lips. Standing exactly opposite to me, on the starboard side, was the mysterious being whom I had last seen in the railway carriage at Sittingbourne. He was, as usual, imperturbable, sardonic, terrifying. His face, which chanced to be lighted by the rays of a deck lantern, had the pallor and the immobility of marble, and the dark eyes held me under their hypnotic gaze.

Again I had the sensation of being victimized by a conspiracy of which this implacable man was the head. I endured once more the mental tortures which I had suffered in the railway carriage, and now, as then, I felt helpless and bewildered. It seemed to me that his existence overshadowed mine, and that in some way he was connected with the death of Alresca. Possibly there was a plot, in which the part played by the jealousy of Carlotta Deschamps was only a minor one. Possibly I had unwittingly stepped into a net of subtle intrigue, of the extent of whose boundaries and ramifications I had not the slightest idea. Like one set in the blackness of an unfamiliar chamber, I feared to step forward or backward lest I might encounter some unknown horror.

It may be argued that I must have been in a highly nervous condition in order to be affected in such a manner by the mere sight of a man—a man who had never addressed to me a single word of conversation. Perhaps so. Yet up to that period of my life my temperament and habit of mind had been calm, unimpressionable, and if I may say so, not specially absurd.

What need to inquire how the man had got on board that ship—how he had escaped death in the railway accident—how he had eluded my sight at Dover Priory? There he stood. Evidently he had purposed to pursue me to Paris, and little things like railway collisions were insufficient to deter him. I surmised that he must have quitted the compartment at Sittingbourne immediately after me, meaning to follow me, but that the starting of the train had prevented him from entering the same compartment as I entered. According to this theory, he must have jumped into another compartment lower down the train as the train was moving, and left it when the collision occurred, keeping his eye on me all the time, but not coming forward. He must even have walked after me down the line from Dover Priory to the pier.

However, a shipwreck was a more serious affair than a railway accident. And if the ship were indeed doomed, it would puzzle even him to emerge with his life. He might seize me in the water, and from simple hate drag me to destruction—yes, that was just what he would do,—but he would have a difficulty in saving himself. Such were my wild and fevered notions!

On the starboard bow I saw the dim bulk and the masthead lights of a steamer approaching us. The other passengers had observed it, too, and there was a buzz of anticipation on the slanting deck. Only the inimical man opposite to me seemed to ignore the stir. He did not even turn round to look at the object which had aroused the general excitement. His eyes never left me.

The vessel came nearer, till we could discern clearly the outline of her, and a black figure on her bridge. She was not more than a hundred yards away when the beat of her engines stopped. She hailed us. We waited for the answering call from our own captain, but there was no reply. Twice again she hailed us, and was answered only by silence.

"Why don't our people reply?" an old lady asked, who came up to me at that moment, breathing heavily.

"Because they are d——d fools," I said roughly. She was a most respectable and prim old lady; yet I could not resist shocking her ears by an impropriety.

The other ship moved away into the night.

Was I in a dream? Was this a pantomime shipwreck? Then it occurred to me that the captain was so sure of being ultimately able to help himself that he preferred from motives of economy to decline assistance which would involve a heavy salvage claim.

My self-possessed young man came along again in the course of his peregrinations, the girl whom he called Lottie still on his arm. He stopped for a chat.

"Most curious thing!" he began.

"What now?"

"Well, I found out about the collision."

"How did it occur?"

"In this way. The captain was on duty on the bridge, with the steersman at the wheel. It was thickish weather then, much thicker than it is now—in fact, there'll soon be no breeze left, and look at the stars! Suddenly the lookout man shouted that there was a sail on the weather bow, and it must have been pretty close, too. The captain ordered the man at the wheel to put the boat to port—I don't know the exact phraseology of the thing—so that we could pass the other ship on our starboard side. Instead of doing that, the triple idiot shoved us to starboard as hard as he could, and before the captain could do anything, we were struck on the port paddle. The steersman had sent us right into the other ship. If he had wanted specially to land us into a good smash-up, he could scarcely have done it better. A good thing we got caught on the paddle; otherwise we should have been cut clean in two. As it was, the other boat recoiled and fell away."

"Was she damaged?"

"Probably not."

"How does the man at the wheel explain his action?"

"Well, that's the curious part. I was just coming to that. Naturally he's in a great state of terror just now, but he can just talk. He swears that when the captain gave his order a third person ran up the steps leading to the bridge, and so frightened him that he was sort of dazed, and did exactly the wrong thing."

"A queer tale!"

"I should think so. But he sticks to it. He even says that this highly mysterious third person made him do the wrong thing. But that's absolute tommy-rot."

"The man must be mad."

"I should have said he had been drunk, but there doesn't seem to be any trace of that. Anyhow, he sees visions, and I maintain that the Chatham and Dover people oughtn't to have their boats steered by men who see visions, eh?"

"I agree with you. I suppose we aren't now in any real danger?"

"I should hardly think so. We might have been. It was pure luck that we happened to get struck on the paddle-box, and also it was pure luck that the sea has gone down so rapidly. With a list like this, a really lively cross-sea would soon have settled us."

We were silent for a few moments. The girl looked idly round the ship, and her eyes encountered the figure of the mysterious man. She seemed to shiver.

"Oh!" she exclaimed under her breath, "what a terrible face that man has!"

"Where?" said her friend.

"Over there. And how is it he's wearing a silk hat—here?"

His glance followed hers, but my follower had turned abruptly round, and in a moment was moving quickly to the after-part of the ship. He passed behind the smoke-stack, and was lost to our view.

"The back of him looks pretty stiff," the young man said. "I wonder if he's the chap that alarmed the man at the wheel."

I laughed, and at the same time I accidentally dropped Rosa's jewel-case, which had never left my hand. I picked it up hurriedly.

"You seem attached to that case," the young man said, smiling. "If we had foundered, should you have let it go, or tried to swim ashore with it?"

"The question is doubtful," I replied, returning his smile. In shipwrecks one soon becomes intimate with strangers.

"If I mistake not, it is a jewel-case."

"It is a jewel-case."

He nodded with a moralizing air, as if reflecting upon the sordid love of property which will make a man carry a jewel-case about with him when the next moment he might find himself in the sea. At least, that was my interpretation of the nodding. Then the brother and sister—for such I afterwards discovered they were—left me to take care of my jewel-case alone.

Why had I dropped the jewel-case? Was it because I was startled by the jocular remark which identified the mysterious man with the person who had disturbed the steersman? That remark was made in mere jest. Yet I could not help thinking that it contained the truth. Nay, I knew that it was true; I knew by instinct. And being true, what facts were logically to be deduced from it? What aim had this mysterious man in compelling, by his strange influences, the innocent sailor to guide the ship towards destruction—the ship in which I happened to be a passenger? … And then there was the railway accident. The stoker had said that the engine-driver had been dazed—like the steersman. But no. There are avenues of conjecture from which the mind shrinks. I could not follow up that train of thought.

Happily, I did not see my enemy again—at least, during that journey. And my mind was diverted, for the dawn came—the beautiful September dawn. Never have I greeted the sun with deeper joy, and I fancy that my sentiments were shared by everyone on board the vessel. As the light spread over the leaden waters, and the coast of France was silhouetted against the sky, the passengers seemed to understand that danger was over, and that we had been through peril, and escaped. Some threw themselves upon their knees, and prayed with an ecstasy of thankfulness. Others re-commenced their hymning. Others laughed rather hysterically, and began to talk at a prodigious rate. A few, like myself, stood silent and apparently unmoved.

Then the engines began to beat. There was a frightful clatter of scrap-iron and wood in the port paddle-box, and they stopped immediately, whereupon we noticed that the list of the vessel was somewhat more marked than before. The remainder of the port paddle had, in fact, fallen away into the water. The hymn-singers ceased their melodies, absorbed in anticipating what would happen next. At last, after many orders and goings to and fro, the engines started again, this time, of course, the starboard paddle, deeply immersed, moved by itself. We progressed with infinite slowness, and in a most peculiar manner, but we did progress, and that was the main thing. The passengers cheered heartily.

We appeared to go in curves, but each curve brought us nearer to Calais. As we approached that haven of refuge, it seemed as if every steamer and smack of Calais was coming out to meet us. The steamers whistled, the owners of smacks bawled and shouted. They desired to assist; for were we not disabled, and would not the English railway company pay well for help so gallantly rendered? Our captain, however, made no sign, and, like a wounded, sullen animal, from whom its companions timidly keep a respectful distance, we at length entered Calais harbour, and by dint of much seamanship and polyglottic swearing brought up safely at the quay.

Then it was that one fully perceived, with a feeling of shame, how night had magnified the seriousness of the adventure; how it had been nothing, after all; how it would not fill more than half a column in the newspapers; how the officers of the ship must have despised the excited foolishness of passengers who would not listen to reasonable, commonplace explanations.

The boat was evacuated in the twinkling of an eye. I have never seen a Channel steamer so quickly empty itself. It was as though the people were stricken by a sudden impulse to dash away from the poor craft at any cost. At the Customs, amid all the turmoil and bustle, I saw neither my young friend and his sister, nor my enemy, who so far had clung to me on my journey.

I learned that a train would start in about a quarter of an hour. I had some coffee and a roll at the buffet. While I was consuming that trifling refection the young man and his sister joined me. The girl was taciturn as before, but her brother talked cheerfully as he sipped chocolate; he told me that his name was Watts, and he introduced his sister. He had a pleasant but rather weak face, and as for his manner and bearing, I could not decide in my own mind whether he was a gentleman or a buyer from some London drapery warehouse on his way to the city of modes. He gave no information as to his profession or business, and as I had not even returned his confidence by revealing my name, this was not to be wondered at.

"Are you going on to Paris?" he said presently.

"Yes; and the sooner I get there the better I shall be pleased."

"Exactly," he smiled. "I am going, too. I have crossed the Channel many times, but I have never before had such an experience as last night's."

Then we began to compare notes of previous voyages, until a railway official entered the buffet with a raucous, "Voyageurs pour Paris, en voiture."

There was only one first-class carriage, and into this I immediately jumped, and secured a corner. Mr Watts followed me, and took the other corner of the same seat. Miss Watts remained on the platform. It was a corridor carriage, and the corridor happened to be on the far side from the platform. Mr Watts went out to explore the corridor. I arranged myself in my seat, placed the jewel-case by my side, and my mackintosh over my knees. Miss Watts stood idly in front of the carriage door, tapping the platform with her umbrella.

"You do not accompany your brother, then?" I ventured.

"No. I'm staying in Calais, where I have an—an engagement." She smiled plaintively at me.

Mr Watts came back into the compartment, and, standing on the step, said good-by to his sister, and embraced her. She kissed him affectionately. Then, having closed the carriage door, he stolidly resumed his seat, which was on the other side away from the door. We had the compartment to ourselves.

"A nice girl," I reflected.

The train whistled, and a porter ran along to put the catches on all the doors.

"Good-by; we're off," I said to Miss Watts.

"Monsieur," she said, and her face seemed to flush in the cold morning light,—"monsieur." Was she, then, French, to address me like that?

She made a gesture as if she would say something to me of importance, and I put my head out of the window.

"May I ask you to keep an eye on my brother?" she whispered.

"In what way?" I asked, somewhat astonished.

The train began to move, and she walked to keep level with me.

"Do not let him drink at any of the railway buffets on the journey; he will be met at the Gare du Nord. He is addicted—"

"But how can I stop him if he wants to—"

She had an appealing look, and she was running now to keep pace with the train.

"Ah, do what you can, sir. I ask it as a favour. Pardon the request from a perfect stranger."

I nodded acquiescence, and, waving a farewell to the poor girl, sank back into my seat. "This is a nice commission!" I thought.

Mr Watts was no longer in his corner. Also my jewel-case was gone.

"A deliberate plant!" I exclaimed; and I could not help admiring the cleverness with which it had been carried out.

I rushed into the corridor, and looked through every compartment; but Mr Watts, whom I was to keep from drunkenness, had utterly departed. Then I made for the handle of the communication cord. It had been neatly cut off. The train was now travelling at a good speed, and the first stop would be Amiens. I was too ashamed of my simplicity to give the news of my loss to the other passengers in the carriage.

"Very smart indeed!" I murmured, sitting down, and I smiled—for, after all, I could afford to smile.

XI

A CHAT WITH ROSA

"And when I sat down it was gone, and the precious Mr Watts had also vanished."

"Oh!" exclaimed Rosa. That was all she said. It is impossible to deny that she was startled, that she was aghast. I, however, maintained a splendid equanimity.

We were sitting in the salon of her flat at the Place de la Concorde end of the Rue de Rivoli. We had finished lunch, and she had offered me a cigarette. I had had a bath, and changed my attire, and eaten a meal cooked by a Frenchman, and I felt renewed. I had sunned myself in the society of Rosetta Rosa for an hour, and I felt soothed. I forgot all the discomforts and misgivings of the voyage. It was nothing to me, as I looked at this beautiful girl, that within the last twenty-four hours I had twice been in danger of losing my life. What to me was the mysterious man with the haunting face of implacable hate? What to me were the words of the woman who had stopped me on the pier at Dover? Nothing! A thousand times less than nothing! I loved, and I was in the sympathetic presence of her whom I loved.

I had waited till lunch was over to tell Rosa of the sad climax of my adventures.

"Yes," I repeated, "I was never more completely done in my life. The woman conspirator took me in absolutely."

"What did you do then?"

"Well, I wired to Calais immediately we got to Amiens, and told the police, and did all the things one usually does do when one has been robbed. Also, since arriving in Paris, I have been to the police here."

"Do they hold out any hope of recovery?"

"I'm afraid they are not sanguine. You see, the pair had a good start, and I expect they belong to one of the leading gangs of jewel thieves in Europe. The entire business must have been carefully planned. Probably I was shadowed from the moment I left your bankers'."

"It's unfortunate."

"Yes, indeed. I felt sure that you would attach some importance to the jewel-case. So I have instructed the police to do their utmost."

She seemed taken aback by the lightness of my tone.

"My friend, those jewels were few, but they were valuable. They were worth—I don't know what they *were* worth. There was a necklace that must have cost fifteen thousand pounds."

"Yes—the jewels."

"Well! Is it not the jewels that are missing?"

"Dear lady," I said, "I aspire to be thought a man of the world—it is a failing of youth; but, then, I am young. As a man of the world, I cogitated a pretty good long time before I set out for Paris with your jewels."

"You felt there was a danger of robbery?"

"Exactly."

"And you were not mistaken." There was irony in her voice.

"True! But let me proceed. A man of the world would see at once that a jewel-case was an object to attract the eyes of those who live by their wits."

"I should imagine so."

"Therefore, as a man of the world, I endeavoured to devise a scheme of safeguarding my little cargo."

"And you—"

"I devised one."

"What was it?"

"I took all the jewels out of the case, and put them into my various pockets; and I carried the case to divert attention from those pockets."

She looked at me, her face at first all perplexity; gradually the light broke upon her.

"Simple, wasn't it?" I murmured.

"Then the jewels are not stolen?"

"Certainly not. The jewels are in my pockets. If you recollect, I said it was the jewel-case that was stolen."

I began to smile.

"Mr Foster," she said, smiling too, "I am extremely angry."

"Forgive the joke," I entreated. "Perhaps it is a bad one—but I hope not a very bad one, because very bad jokes are inexcusable. And here are your jewels."

I put on the expression of a peccant but hopeful schoolboy, as I emptied one pocket after another of the scintillating treasures. The jewels lay, a gorgeous heap, on her lap. The necklace which she had particularly mentioned was of pearls. There were also rubies and emeralds, upon which she seemed to set special store, and a brooch in the form of a butterfly, which she said was made expressly for her by Lalique. But not a diamond in the collection! It appeared that she regarded diamonds as some men regard champagne—as a commodity not appealing to the very finest taste.

"I didn't think you were so mischievous," she laughed, frowning.

To transfer the jewels to her possession I had drawn my chair up to hers, and we were close together, face to face.

"Ah!" I replied, content, unimaginably happy. "You don't know me yet. I'm a terrible fellow."

"Think of my state of mind during the last fifteen minutes."

"Yes, but think of the joy which you now experience. It is I who have given you that joy—the joy of losing and gaining all that in a quarter of an hour."

She picked up the necklace, and as she gazed at the stones her glance had a rapt expression, as though she were gazing through their depths into the past.

"Mr Foster," she said at length, without ceasing to look at the pearls, "I cannot tell you how glad I am that you are in Paris. Shall you stay till I have appeared at the Opéra Comique?"

"I was hoping to, and if you say you would like me to—"

"Ah!" she exclaimed, "I do." And she looked up.

Her lovely eyes had a suspicion of moisture. The blood rushed through my head, and I could feel its turbulent throb-throb across the temples and at my heart.

I was in heaven, and residence in heaven makes one bold.

"You really would like me to stay?" I almost whispered, in a tone that was equivalent to a declaration.

Her eyes met mine in silence for a few instants, and then she said, with a touch of melancholy:

"In all my life I've only had two friends—I mean since my mother's death; and you are the third."

"Is that all?"

"You don't know what a life like mine is," she went on, with feeling. "I'm only a *prima donna*, you know. People think that because I can make as much money in three hours as a milliner's girl can make in three years, and because I'm always in the midst of luxuries, and because I have whims and caprices, and because my face has certain curves in it, and because men get jealous with each other about kissing my hand, that therefore I've got all I want."

"Certain curves!" I burst out. "Why, you're the most beautiful creature I ever saw!"

"There!" she cried. "That's just how they all talk. I do hate it."

"Do you?" I said. "Then I'll never call you beautiful again. But I should have thought you were fairly happy."

"I'm happy when I'm singing well," she answered—"only then. I like singing. I like to see an audience moved. I must sing. Singing is my life. But do you know what that means? That means that I belong to the public, and so I can't hide myself. That means that I am always—always—surrounded by 'admirers.'"

"Well?"

"Well, I don't like them. I don't like any of them. And I don't like them in the mass. Why can't I just sing, and then belong simply to myself? They are for ever there, my 'admirers.' Men of wealth, men of talent, men of adventure, men of wits—all devoted, all respectful, all ready to marry me. Some honourable, according to the accepted standard, others probably dishonourable. And there is not one but whose real desire is to own me. I know them. Love! In my world, peculiar in that world in which I live, there is no such thing as love—only a showy imitation. Yes, they think they love me. 'When we are married you will not sing any more; you will be mine then,' says one. That is what he imagines is love. And others would have me for the gold-mine that is in my throat. I can read their greed in their faces."

Her candid bitterness surprised as much as it charmed me.

"Aren't you a little hard on them?" I ventured.

"Now, am I?" she retorted. "Don't be a hypocrite. Am I?"

I said nothing.

"You know perfectly well I'm not," she answered for me.

"But *I* admire you," I said.

"You're different," she replied. "You don't belong to my world. That's what pleases me in you. You haven't got that silly air of always being ready to lay down your life for me. You didn't come in this morning with a bunch of expensive orchids, and beg that I should deign to accept them." She pointed to various bouquets in the room. "You just came in and shook hands, and asked me how I was."

"I never thought of bringing any flowers," I said awkwardly.

"Just so. That's the point. That's what I like. If there is one thing that I can't tolerate, and that I *have* to tolerate, it's 'attentions,' especially from people who copy their deportment from Russian Archdukes."

"There are Archdukes?"

"Why! the air is thick with them. Why do men think that a woman is flattered by their ridiculous 'attentions?' If they knew how sometimes I can scarcely keep from laughing! There are moments when I would give anything to be back again in the days when I knew no one more distinguished than a concierge. There was more sincerity at my disposal then."

"But surely all distinguished people are not insincere?"

"They are insincere to opera singers who happen to be young, beautiful, and rich, which is my sad case. The ways of the people who flutter round a theatre are not my ways. I was brought up simply, as you were in your Devonshire home. I hate to spend my life as if it was one long diplomatic reception. Ugh!"

She clenched her hands, and one of the threads of the necklace gave way, and the pearls scattered themselves over her lap.

"There! That necklace was given to me by one of my friends!" She paused.

"Yes?" I said tentatively.

"He is dead now. You have heard—everyone knows—that I was once engaged to Lord Clarenceux. He *was* a friend. He loved me—he died—my friends have a habit of dying. Alresca died."

The conversation halted. I wondered whether I might speak of Lord Clarenceux, or whether to do so would be an indiscretion. She began to collect the pearls.

"Yes," she repeated softly, "*he* was a friend."

I drew a strange satisfaction from the fact that, though she had said frankly that he loved her, she had not even hinted that she loved him.

"Lord Clarenceux must have been a great man," I said.

"That is exactly what he was," she answered with a vague enthusiasm. "And a great nobleman too! So different from the others. I wish I could describe him to you, but I cannot. He was immensely rich—he looked on me as a pauper. He had the finest houses, the finest judgment in the world. When he wanted anything he got it, no matter what the cost. All dealers knew that, and anyone who had 'the best' to sell knew that in Lord Clarenceux he would find a purchaser. He carried things with a high hand. I never knew another man so determined, or one who could be more stern or more exquisitely kind. He knew every sort of society, and yet he had never married. He fell in love with me, and offered me his hand. I declined—I was afraid of him. He said he would shoot himself. And he would have done it; so I accepted. I should have ended by loving him. For he wished me to love him, and he always had his way. He was a man, and he held the same view of my world that I myself hold. Mr Foster, you must think I'm in a very chattering mood."

I protested with a gesture.

"Lord Clarenceux died. And I am alone. I was terribly lonely after his death. I missed his jealousy."

"He was jealous?"

"He was the most jealous man, I think, who ever lived. His jealousy escorted me everywhere like a guard of soldiers. Yet I liked him even for that. He was genuine; so sincere, so masterful with it. In all matters his methods were drastic. If he had been alive I should not be tormented by the absurd fears which I now allow to get the better of me."

"Fears! About what?"

"To be frank, about my debut at the Opéra Comique. I can imagine," she smiled, "how he would have dealt with that situation."

"You are afraid of something?"

"Yes."

"What is it?"

"I don't know. I merely fear … There is Carlotta Deschamps."

"Miss Rosa, a few minutes ago you called me your friend." My voice was emotional; I felt it.

"I did, because you are. I have no claim on you, but you have been very good to me."

"You have the best claim on me. Will you rely on me?"

We looked at each other.

"I will," she said. I stood before her, and she took my hand.

"You say you fear. I hope your fears are groundless—candidly, I can't see how they can be otherwise. But suppose anything should happen. Well, I shall be at your service."

At that moment someone knocked and entered. It was Yvette. She avoided my glance.

"Madame will take her egg-and-milk before going to rehearsal?"

"Yes, Yvette. Bring it to me here, please."

"You have a rehearsal to-day?" I asked. "I hope I'm not detaining you."

"Not at all. The call is for three o'clock. This is the second one, and they fixed the hour to suit me. It is really my first rehearsal, because at the previous one I was too hoarse to sing a note."

I rose to go.

"Wouldn't you like to come with me to the theatre?" she said with an adorable accent of invitation.

My good fortune staggered me.

After she had taken her egg-and-milk we set out.

XII

EGG-AND-MILK

I WAS INTENSELY CONSCIOUS OF her beauty as I sat by her side in the swiftly rolling victoria. And I was conscious of other qualities in her too—of her homeliness, her good-fellowship, her trustfulness. The fact that she was one of the most famous personalities in Europe did not, after our talk, in the least disturb my pleasing dreams of a possible future. It was, nevertheless, specially forced upon me, for as we drove along the Rue de Rivoli, past the interminable façades of the Louvre, and the big shops, and so into the meaner quarter of the markets—the Opéra Comique was then situated in its temporary home in the Place du Châtelet—numberless wayfarers showed by their demeanour of curiosity that Rosetta Rosa was known to them. They were much more polite than English people would have been, but they did not hide their interest in us.

The jewels had been locked away in a safe, except one gorgeous emerald brooch which she was wearing at her neck.

"It appears," I said, "that in Paris one must not even attend rehearsals without jewels."

She laughed.

"You think I have a passion for jewels, and you despise me for it."

"By no means. Nobody has a better right to wear precious stones than yourself."

"Can you guess why I wear them?"

"Not because they make you look prettier, for that's impossible."

"Will you please remember that I like you because you are not in the habit of making speeches."

"I beg pardon. I won't offend again. Well, then, I will confess that I don't know why you wear jewels. There must be a Puritan strain in my character, for I cannot enter into the desire for jewels. I say this merely because you have practically invited me to be brutal."

Now that I recall that conversation I realize how gentle she was towards my crude and callous notions concerning personal adornment.

"Yet you went to England in order to fetch my jewels."

"No, I went to England in order to be of use to a lady. But tell me—why do you wear jewels off the stage?"

"Simply because, having them, I have a sort of feeling that they ought to be used. It seems a waste to keep them hidden in a strong box, and I never could tolerate waste. Really, I scarcely care more for jewels, as jewels, than you do yourself."

"Still, for a person who doesn't care for them, you seem to have a fair quantity of them."

"Ah! But many were given to me—and the rest I bought when I was young, or soon afterwards. Besides, they are part of my stock in trade."

"When you were young!" I repeated, smiling. "How long is that since?"

"Ages."

I coughed.

"It is seven years since I was young," she said, "and I was sixteen at the time."

"You are positively venerable, then; and since you are, I must be too."

"I am much older than you are," she said; "not in years, but in life. You don't feel old."

"And do you?"

"Frightfully."

"What brings it on?"

"Oh! Experience—and other things. It is the soul which grows old."

"But you have been happy?"

"Never—never in my life, except when I was singing, have I been happy. Have you been happy?"

"Yes," I said, "once or twice."

"When you were a boy?"

"No, since I have become a man. Just—just recently."

"People fancy they are happy," she murmured.

"Isn't that the same thing as being happy?"

"Perhaps." Then suddenly changing the subject: "You haven't told me about your journey. Just a bare statement that there was a delay on the railway and another delay on the steamer. Don't you think you ought to fill in the details?"

So I filled them in; but I said nothing about my mysterious enemy who had accompanied me, and who after strangely disappearing and reappearing had disappeared again; nor about the woman whom I had met on the Admiralty Pier. I wondered when he might reappear once more. There was no proper reason why I should not have told Rosa about these persons, but some instinctive feeling, some timidity of spirit, prevented me from doing so.

"How thrilling! Were you frightened on the steamer?" she asked.

"Yes," I admitted frankly.

"You may not think it," she said, "but I should not have been frightened. I have never been frightened at Death."

"But have you ever been near him?"

"Who knows?" she answered thoughtfully.

We were at the stage-door of the theatre. The olive-liveried footman dismounted, and gravely opened the door of the carriage. I got out, and gave my hand to Rosa, and we entered the theatre.

In an instant she had become the *prima donna*. The curious little officials of the theatre bowed before her, and with prodigious smiles waved us forward to the stage. The stage-manager, a small, fat man with white hair, was drilling the chorus. As soon as he caught sight of us he dismissed the short-skirted girls and the fatigued-looking men, and skipped towards us. The orchestra suddenly ceased. Everyone was quiet. The star had come.

"Good day, mademoiselle. You are here to the moment."

Rosa and the *régisseur* talked rapidly together, and presently the conductor of the orchestra stepped from his raised chair on to the stage, and with a stately inclination to Rosa joined in the conversation. As for me, I looked about, and was stared at. So far as I could see there was not much difference between an English stage and a French stage, viewed at close quarters, except that the French variety possesses perhaps more officials and a more bureaucratic air. I gazed into the cold, gloomy auditorium, so bare of decoration, and decided that in England such an auditorium would not be tolerated.

After much further chatter the conductor bowed again, and returned to his seat. Rosa beckoned to me, and I was introduced to the stage-manager.

"Allow me to present to you Mr Foster, one of my friends."

Rosa coughed, and I noticed that her voice was slightly hoarse.

"You have taken cold during the drive," I said, pouring into the sea of French a little stream of English.

"Oh, no. It is nothing; it will pass off in a minute."

The stage-manager escorted me to a chair near a grand piano which stood in the wings. Then some male artists, evidently people of importance, appeared out of the darkness at the back of the stage. Rosa took off her hat and gloves, and placed them on the grand piano. I observed that she was flushed, and I put it down to the natural excitement of the artist about to begin work. The orchestra sounded resonantly in the empty theatre, and, under the yellow glare of unshaded electricity, the rehearsal of *Carmen* began at the point where Carmen makes her first entry.

As Rosa came to the centre of the stage from the wings she staggered. One would have thought she was drunk. At her cue, instead of commencing to sing, she threw up her hands, and with an appealing glance at me sank down to the floor. I rushed to her, and immediately the entire *personnel* of the theatre was in a state of the liveliest excitement.

I thought of a similar scene in London not many months before. But the poor girl was perfectly conscious, and even self-possessed.

"Water!" she murmured. "I shall die of thirst if you don't give me some water to drink at once."

There appeared to be no water within the theatre, but at last someone appeared with a carafe and glass. She drank two glassfuls, and then dropped the glass, which broke on the floor.

"I am not well," she said; "I feel so hot, and there is that hoarseness in my throat. Mr Foster, you must take me home. The rehearsal will have to be postponed again; I am sorry. It's very queer."

She stood up with my assistance, looking wildly about her, but appealing to no one but myself.

"It is queer," I said, supporting her.

"Mademoiselle was ill in the same way last time," several sympathetic voices cried out, and some of the women caressed her gently.

"Let me get home," she said, half-shouting, and she clung to me. "My hat—my gloves—quick!"

"Yes, yes," I said; "I will get a fiacre."

"Why not my victoria?" she questioned imperiously.

"Because you must go in a closed carriage," I said firmly.

"Mademoiselle will accept my brougham?"

A tall dark man had come forward. He was the Escamillo. She thanked him with a look. Some woman threw a cloak over Rosa's shoulders, and, the baritone on one side of her and myself on the other, we left the theatre. It seemed scarcely a moment since she had entered it confident and proud.

During the drive back to her flat I did not speak, but I examined her narrowly. Her skin was dry and burning, and on her forehead there was a slight rash. Her lips were dry, and she continually made the motion of swallowing. Her eyes sparkled, and they seemed to stand out from her head. Also she still bitterly complained of thirst. She wanted, indeed, to stop the carriage and have something to drink at the Café de l'Univers, but I absolutely declined to permit such a proceeding, and in a few minutes we were at her flat. The attack was passing away. She mounted the stairs without much difficulty.

"You must go to bed," I said. We were in the salon. "In a few hours you will be better."

"I will ring for Yvette."

"No," I said, "you will not ring for Yvette. I want Yvette myself. Have you no other servant who can assist you?"

"Yes. But why not Yvette?"

"You can question me to-morrow. Please obey me now. I am your doctor. I will ring the bell. Yvette will come, and you will at once go out of the room, find another servant, and retire to bed. You can do that? You are not faint?"

"No, I can do it; but it is very queer."

I rang the bell.

"You have said that before, and I say, 'It is queer; queerer than you imagine.' One thing I must ask you before you go. When you had the attack in the theatre did you see things double?"

"Yes," she answered. "But how did you know? I felt as though I was intoxicated; but I had taken nothing whatever."

"Excuse me, you had taken egg-and-milk. Here is the glass out of which you drank it." I picked up the glass, which had been left on the table, and which still contained about a spoonful of egg-and-milk.

Yvette entered in response to my summons.

"Mademoiselle has returned soon," the girl began lightly.

"Yes."

The two women looked at each other. I hastened to the door, and held it open for Rosa to pass out. She did so. I closed the door, and put my back against it. The glass I still held in my hand.

"Now, Yvette, I want to ask you a few questions."

She stood before me, pretty even in her plain black frock and black apron, and folded her hands. Her face showed no emotion whatever.

"Yes, monsieur, but mademoiselle will need me."

"Mademoiselle will not need you. She will never need you again."

"Monsieur says?"

"You see this glass. What did you put in it?"

"The cook put egg-and-milk into it."

"I ask what you put in it?"

"I, monsieur? Nothing."

"You are lying, my girl. Your mistress has been poisoned."

"I swear—"

"I should advise you not to swear. You have twice attempted to poison your mistress. Why did you do it?"

"But this is absurd."

"Does your mistress use eyedrops when she sings at the Opéra?"

"Eyedrops?"

"You know what I mean. A lotion which you drop into the eye in order to dilate the pupil."

"My mistress never uses eyedrops."

"Does Madame Carlotta Deschamps use eyedrops?"

It was a courageous move on my part, but it had its effect. She was startled.

"I—I don't know, monsieur."

"I ask because eyedrops contain atropine, and mademoiselle is suffering from a slight, a very slight, attack of atropine poisoning. The dose must have been very nicely gauged; it was just enough to produce a temporary hoarseness and discomfort. I needn't tell such a clever girl as you that atropine acts first on the throat. It has clearly been someone's intention to prevent mademoiselle from singing at rehearsals, and from appearing in Paris in *Carmen*."

Yvette drew herself up, her nostrils quivering. She had turned decidedly pale.

"Monsieur insults me by his suspicions. I must go."

"You won't go just immediately. I may tell you further that I have analyzed the contents of this glass, and have found traces of atropine."

I had done no such thing, but that was a detail.

"Also, I have sent for the police."

This, too, was an imaginative statement.

Yvette approached me suddenly, and flung her arms round my neck. I had just time to put the glass on the seat of a chair and seize her hands.

"No," I said, "you will neither spill that glass nor break it."

She dropped at my feet weeping.

"Have pity on me, monsieur!" She looked up at me through her tears, and the pose was distinctly effective. "It was Madame Deschamps who asked me to do it. I used to be with her before I came to mademoiselle. She gave me the bottle, but I didn't know it was poison—I swear I didn't!"

"What did you take it to be, then? Jam? Two grains of atropine will cause death."

For answer she clung to my knees. I released myself, and moved away a few steps. She jumped up, and made a dash for the door, but I happened to have locked it.

"Where is Madame Deschamps?" I asked.

"She returns to Paris to-morrow. Monsieur will let me go. I was only a tool."

"I will consider that matter, Yvette," I said. "In my opinion you are a thoroughly wicked girl, and I wouldn't trust you any further than I could see you. For the present, you will have an opportunity to meditate over your misdoings." I left the room, and locked the door on the outside.

Impossible to disguise the fact that I was enormously pleased with myself—with my sharpness, my smartness, my penetration, my success.

XIII

THE PORTRAIT

FOR THE NEXT HOUR OR two I wandered about Rosa's flat like an irresolute and bewildered spirit. I wished to act, yet without Rosa I scarcely liked to do so. That some sort of a plot existed—whether serious or trivial was no matter—there could be little doubt, and there could be little doubt also that Carlotta Deschamps was at the root of it.

Several half-formed schemes flitted through my head, but none of them seemed to be sufficiently clever. I had the idea of going to see Carlotta Deschamps in order to warn her. Then I thought the warning might perhaps be sent through her sister Marie, who was doubtless in Paris, and who would probably be able to control Carlotta. I had not got Carlotta's address, but I might get it by going to the Casino de Paris, and asking Marie for it. Perhaps Marie, suspicious, might refuse the address. Had she not said that she and Carlotta were as thick as thieves? Moreover, assuming that I could see Carlotta, what should I say to her? How should I begin? Then it occurred to me that the shortest way with such an affair was to go directly to the police, as I had already threatened Yvette; but the appearance of the police would mean publicity, scandal, and other things unpleasant for Rosa. So it fell out that I maintained a discreet inactivity.

Towards nightfall I went into the street to breathe the fresh air. A man was patrolling the pavement in a somewhat peculiar manner. I returned indoors, and after half an hour reconnoitred once more. The man was on the opposite side of the road, with his eyes on the windows of the salon. When he caught sight of me he walked slowly away. He might have been signalling to Yvette, who was still under lock and key, but this possibility did not disturb me, as escape was out of the question for her.

I went back to the flat, and a servant met me in the hall with a message that mademoiselle was now quite recovered, and would like to see me in her boudoir. I hurried to her. A fire was burning on the hearth, and before this were two lounge chairs. Rosa occupied one, and she motioned me to the other. Attired in a peignoir of pure white, and still a little languorous after the attack, she looked the enchanting perfection of beauty and grace. But in her eyes, which were unduly bright, there shone an apprehension, the expectancy of the unknown.

"I am better," she said, with a faint smile. "Feel my pulse."

I held her wrist and took out my watch, but I forgot to count, and I forgot to note the seconds. I was gazing at her. It seemed absurd to contemplate the possibility of ever being able to call her my own.

"Am I not better?"

"Yes, yes," I said; "the pulse is—the pulse is—you are much better."

Then I pushed my chair a little further from the fire, and recollected that there were several things to be said and done.

"I expected the attack would pass very quickly," I said.

"Then you know what I have been suffering from," she said, turning her chair rapidly half-round towards me.

"I do," I answered, with emphasis.

"What is it?"

I was silent.

"Well," she said, "tell me what it is." She laughed, but her voice was low and anxious.

"I am just wondering whether I *shall* tell you."

"Stuff!" she exclaimed proudly. "Am I a child?"

"You are a woman, and should be shielded from the sharp edges of life."

"Ah!" she murmured "Not all men have thought so. And I wish you wouldn't talk like that."

"Nevertheless, I think like that," I said. "And I'm really anxious to save you from unnecessary annoyance."

"Then I insist that you shall tell me," she replied inconsequently. "I will not have you adopt that attitude towards me. Do you understand? I won't have it! I'm not a Dresden shepherdess, and I won't be treated like one—at any rate, by you. So there!"

I was in the seventh heaven of felicity.

"If you will have it, you have been poisoned."

I told her of my suspicions, and how they had been confirmed by Yvette's avowal. She shivered, and then stood up and came towards me.

"Do you mean to say that Carlotta Deschamps and my own maid have conspired together to poison me simply because I am going to sing in a certain piece at a certain theatre? It's impossible!"

"But it is true. Deschamps may not have wished to kill you; she merely wanted to prevent you from singing, but she ran a serious risk of murder, and she must have known it."

Rosa began to sob, and I led her back to her chair.

"I ought not to have told you to-night," I said. "But we should communicate with the police, and I wanted your authority before doing so."

She dried her eyes, but her frame still shook.

"I will sing *Carmen*," she said passionately.

"Of course you will. We must get these two arrested, and you shall have proper protection."

"Police? No! We will have no police."

"You object to the scandal? I had thought of that."

"It is not that I object to the scandal. I despise Deschamps and Yvette too much to take the slightest notice of either of them. I could not have believed that women would so treat another woman." She hid her face in her hands.

"But is it not your duty—" I began.

"Mr Foster, please, please don't argue. I am incapable of prosecuting these creatures. You say Yvette is locked up in the salon. Go to her, and tell her to depart. Tell her that I shall do nothing, that I do not hate her, that I bear her no ill-will, that I simply ignore her. And let her carry the same message to Carlotta Deschamps."

"Suppose there should be a further plot?"

"There can't be. Knowing that this one is discovered, they will never dare … And even if they tried again in some other way, I would sooner walk in danger all my life than acknowledge the existence of such creatures. Will you go at once?"

"As you wish;" and I went out.

"Mr Foster."

She called me back. Taking my hand with a gesture half-caressing, she raised her face to mine. Our eyes met, and in hers was a gentle, trustful appeal, a pathetic and entrancing wistfulness, which sent a sudden thrill through me. Her clasp of my fingers tightened ever so little.

"I haven't thanked you in words," she said, "for all you have done for me, and are doing. But you know I'm grateful, don't you?"

I could feel the tears coming into my eyes.

"It is nothing, absolutely nothing," I muttered, and hurried from the room.

At first, in the salon, I could not see Yvette, though the electric light had been turned on, no doubt by herself. Then there was a movement of one of the window-curtains, and she appeared from behind it.

"Oh, it is you," she said calmly, with a cold smile. She had completely recovered her self-possession, so much was evident; and apparently she was determined to play the game to the end, accepting defeat with an air of ironical and gay indifference. Yvette was by no means an ordinary woman. Her face was at once sinister and attractive, with lines of strength about it; she moved with a certain distinction; she had brains and various abilities; and I imagined her to have been capable of some large action, a first-class sin or a really dramatic self-sacrifice—she would have been ready for either. But of her origin I am to this day as ignorant as of her ultimate fate.

A current of air told me that a window was open.

"I noticed a suspicious-looking man outside just now," I said. "Is he one of your confederates? Have you been communicating with him?"

She sat down in an armchair, leaned backwards, and began to hum an air—*la, la, la.*

"Answer me. Come!"

"And if I decline?"

"You will do well to behave yourself," I said; and, going to the window, I closed it, and slipped the catch.

"I hope the gendarmes will be here soon," she murmured amiably; "I am rather tired of waiting." She affected to stifle a yawn.

"Yvette," I said, "you know as well as I do that you have committed a serious crime. Tell me all about Deschamps' jealousy of your mistress; make a full confession, and I will see what can be done for you."

She put her thin lips together.

"No," she replied in a sharp staccato. "I have done what I have done, and I will answer only the *juge d'instruction.*"

"Better think twice."

"Never. It is a trick you wish to play on me."

"Very well." I went to the door, and opened it wide. "You are free to go."

"To go?"

"It is your mistress's wish."

"She will not send me to prison?"

"She scorns to do anything whatever."

For a moment the girl looked puzzled, and then:

"Ah! it is a bad pleasantry; the gendarmes are on the stairs."

I shrugged my shoulders, and at length she tripped quietly out of the room. I heard her run down-stairs. Then, to my astonishment, the footfalls approached again, and Yvette re-entered the room and closed the door.

"I see it is not a bad pleasantry," she began, with her back to the door. "Mademoiselle is a great lady, and I have always known that; she is an artist; she has soul—so have I. What you could not force from me, neither you nor any man, I will tell you of my own free will. You want to hear of Deschamps?"

I nodded, half-admiring her—perhaps more than half.

"She is a woman to fear. I have told you I used to be her maid before I came to mademoiselle, and even *I* was always afraid of her. But I liked her. We understood each other, Deschamps and I. Mademoiselle imagines that Deschamps became jealous of her because of a certain affair that happened at the Opéra Comique several years ago—a mere quarrel of artists, of which I have seen many. That was partly the cause, but there was something else. Deschamps used to think that Lord Clarenceux was in love with her—with her! As a fact, he was not; but she used to think so, and when Lord Clarenceux first began to pay attention to mademoiselle, then it was that the jealousy of Deschamps really sprang up. Ah! I have heard Deschamps swear to—But that is nothing. She never forgave mademoiselle for being betrothed to Lord Clarenceux. When he died, she laughed; but her hatred of mademoiselle was unchanged. It smouldered, only it was very hot underneath. And I can understand—Lord Clarenceux was so handsome and so rich, the most fine stern man I ever saw. He used to give me hundred-franc notes."

"Never mind the notes. Why has Deschamps' jealousy revived so suddenly just recently?"

"Why? Because mademoiselle would come back to the Opéra Comique. Deschamps could not suffer that. And when she heard it was to be so, she wrote to me—to me!—and asked if it was true that mademoiselle was to appear as Carmen. Then she came to see me—me—and I was obliged to tell her it was true, and she was frightfully angry, and then she began to cry—oh, her despair! She said she knew a way to stop mademoiselle from singing, and she begged me to help her, and I said I would."

"You were willing to betray your mistress?"

"Deschamps swore it would do no real harm. Do I not tell you that Deschamps and I always liked each other? We were old friends. I sympathized with her; she is growing old."

"How much did she promise to pay you?"

"Not a sou—not a centime. I swear it." The girl stamped her foot and threw up her head, reddening with the earnestness of her disclaimer. "What I did, I did from love; and I thought it would not harm mademoiselle, really."

"Nevertheless you might have killed your mistress."

"Alas!"

"Answer me this: Now that your attempt has failed, what will Deschamps do? Will she stop, or will she try something else?"

Yvette shook her head slowly.

"I do not know. She is dangerous. Sometimes she is like a mad woman. You must take care. For myself, I will never see her again."

"You give your word on that?"

"I have said it. There is nothing more to tell you. So, adieu. Say to mademoiselle that I have repented."

She opened the door, and as she did so her eye seemed by chance to catch a small picture which hung by the side of the hearth. My back was to the fireplace, and I did not trouble to follow her glance.

"Ah," she murmured reflectively, "he was the most fine stern man … and he gave me hundred-franc notes."

Then she was gone. We never saw nor heard of Yvette again.

Out of curiosity, I turned to look at the picture which must have caught her eye. It was a little photograph, framed in black, and hung by itself on the wall; in the ordinary way one would scarcely have noticed it. I went close up to it. My heart gave a jump, and I seemed to perspire. The photograph was a portrait of the man who, since my acquaintance with Rosa, had haunted my footsteps—the mysterious and implacable person whom I had seen first opposite the Devonshire Mansion, then in the cathedral at Bruges during my vigil by the corpse of Alresca, then in the train which was wrecked, and finally in the Channel steamer which came near to sinking. Across the lower part of it ran the signature, in large, stiff characters, 'Clarenceux.'

So Lord Clarenceux was not dead, though everyone thought him so. Here was a mystery more disturbing than anything which had gone before.

XIV

THE VILLA

IT SEEMED TO BE MY duty to tell Rosa, of course with all possible circumspection, that, despite a general impression to the contrary, Lord Clarenceux was still alive. His lordship's reasons for effacing himself, and so completely deceiving his friends and the world, I naturally could not divine; but I knew that such things had happened before, and also I gathered that he was a man who would hesitate at no caprice, however extravagant, once it had suggested itself to him as expedient for the satisfaction of his singular nature.

A light broke in upon me: Alresca must have been aware that Lord Clarenceux was alive. That must have been part of Alresca's secret, but only part. I felt somehow that I was on the verge of some tragical discovery which might vitally affect not only my own existence, but that of others.

I saw Rosa on the morning after my interview with Yvette. She was in perfect health and moderately good spirits, and she invited me to dine with her that evening. "I will tell her after dinner," I said to myself. The project of telling her seemed more difficult as it approached. She said that she had arranged by telephone for another rehearsal at the Opéra Comique at three o'clock, but she did not invite me to accompany her. I spent the afternoon at the Sorbonne, where I had some acquaintances, and after calling at my hotel, the little Hôtel de Portugal in the Rue Croix des Petits Champs, to dress, I drove in a fiacre to the Rue de

Rivoli. I had carefully considered how best in conversation I might lead Rosa to the subject of Lord Clarenceux, and had arranged a little plan. Decidedly I did not anticipate the interview with unmixed pleasure; but, as I have said, I felt bound to inform her that her former lover's death was a fiction. My suit might be doomed thereby to failure,—I had no right to expect otherwise,—but if it should succeed and I had kept silence on this point, I should have played the part of a—well, of a man 'of three letters.'

"Mademoiselle is not at home," said the servant.

"Not at home! But I am dining with her, my friend."

"Mademoiselle has been called away suddenly, and she has left a note for monsieur. Will monsieur give himself the trouble to come into the salon?"

The note ran thus:

> Dear Friend,
> A thousand excuses! But the enclosed will explain. I felt that I must go—and go instantly. She might die before I arrived. Will you call early to-morrow?
> Your grateful
> Rosa.

And this was the enclosure, written in French:

> Villa des Hortensias, Rue Thiers, Pantin, Paris.
> Mademoiselle,
> I am dying. I have wronged you deeply, and I dare not die without your forgiveness. Prove to me that you have a great heart by coming to my bedside and telling me that you accept my repentance. The bearer will conduct you.
> Carlotta Deschamps.

"What time did mademoiselle leave?" I inquired.

"Less than a quarter of an hour ago," was the reply.

"Who brought the note to her?"

"A man, monsieur. Mademoiselle accompanied him in a cab."

With a velocity which must have startled the grave and leisurely servant, I precipitated myself out of the house and back into the fiacre, which happily had not gone away. I told the cabman to drive to my hotel at his best speed.

To me Deschamps' letter was in the highest degree suspicious. Rosa, of course, with the simplicity of a heart incapable of any baseness, had accepted it in perfect faith. But I remembered the words of Yvette, uttered in all solemnity: "She is dangerous; you must take care." Further, I observed that the handwriting of this strange and dramatic missive was remarkably firm and regular for a dying woman, and that the composition showed a certain calculated effectiveness. I feared a lure. Instinctively I knew Deschamps to be one of those women who, driven by the goad of passionate feeling, will proceed to any length, content to postpone reflection till afterwards—when the irremediable has happened.

By chance I was slightly acquainted with the remote and sinister suburb where lay the Villa des Hortensias. I knew that at night it possessed a peculiar reputation, and my surmise was that Rosa had been decoyed thither with some evil intent.

Arrived at my hotel, I unearthed my revolver and put it in my pocket. Nothing might occur; on the other hand, everything might occur, and it was only prudent to be prepared. Dwelling on this thought, I also took the little jewelled dagger which Rosa had given to Sir Cyril Smart at the historic reception of my Cousin Sullivan's.

In the hall of the hotel I looked at the plan of Paris. Certainly Pantin seemed to be a very long way off. The route to it from the centre of the city—that is to say, the Place de l'Opéra—followed the Rue Lafayette, which is the longest straight thoroughfare in Paris, and then the Rue d'Allemagne, which is a continuation, in the same direct line, of the Rue Lafayette. The suburb lay without the fortifications. The Rue Thiers—every Parisian suburb has its Rue Thiers—was about half a mile past the barrier, on the right.

I asked the aged woman who fulfils the functions of hall-porter at the Hôtel de Portugal whether a cab would take me to Pantin.

"Pantin," she repeated, as she might have said "Timbuctoo." And she called the proprietor. The proprietor also said "Pantin" as he might have said "Timbuctoo," and advised me to take the steam-tram which starts from behind the Opéra, to let that carry me as far as it would, and then, arrived in those distant regions, either to find a cab or to walk the remainder of the distance.

So, armed, I issued forth, and drove to the tram, and placed myself on the top of the tram. And the tram, after much tooting of horns, set out.

Through kilometre after kilometre of gaslit clattering monotony that immense and deafening conveyance took me. There were cafés everywhere, thickly strewn on both sides of the way—at first large and lofty and richly decorated, with vast glazed façades, and manned by waiters in black and white, then gradually growing smaller and less busy. The black and white waiters gave place to men in blouses, and men in blouses gave place to women and girls—short, fat women and girls who gossiped among themselves and to customers. Once we passed a café quite deserted save for the waiter and the waitress, who sat, head on arms, side by side, over a table asleep.

Then the tram stopped finally, having covered about three miles. There was no sign of a cab. I proceeded on foot. The shops got smaller and dingier; they were filled, apparently, by the families of the proprietors. At length I crossed over a canal—the dreadful quarter of La Villette—and here the street widened out to an immense width, and it was silent and forlorn under the gas-lamps. I hurried under railway bridges, and I saw in the distance great shunting-yards looking grim in their blue hazes of electric light. Then came the city barrier and the octroi, and still the street stretched in front of me, darker now, more mischievous, more obscure. I was in Pantin.

At last I descried the white and blue sign of the Rue Thiers. I stood alone in the shadow of high, forbidding houses. All seemed strange and fearsome. Certainly this might still be called Paris, but it was not the Paris known to Englishmen; it was the Paris of Zola, and Zola in a Balzacian mood.

I turned into the Rue Thiers, and at once the high, forbidding houses ceased, and small detached villas—such as are to be found in thousands round the shabby skirts of Paris—took their place. The Villa des Hortensias, clearly labelled, was nearly at the far end of the funereal street. It was rather larger than its fellows, and comprised three stories, with a small garden in front and a vast grille with a big bell, such as Parisians love when they have passed the confines of the city, and have dispensed with the security of a concierge. The grille was ajar. I entered the garden, having made sure that the bell would not sound. The façade of the house showed no light whatever. A double stone stairway of four steps led to the front door. I went up the steps, and was about to knock, when the idea flashed across my mind: "Suppose that Deschamps is really dying, how am I to explain my presence here? I am not the guardian of Rosa, and she may resent being tracked across Paris by a young man with no claim to watch her actions."

Nevertheless, in an expedition of this nature one must accept risks, and therefore I knocked gently. There was no reply to the summons, and I was cogitating upon my next move when, happening to press against the door with my hand, I discovered that it was not latched. Without weighing consequences, I quietly opened it, and with infinite caution stepped into the hall, and pushed the door to. I did not latch it, lest I might need to make a sudden exit—unfamiliar knobs and springs are apt to be troublesome when one is in a hurry.

I was now fairly in the house, but the darkness was blacker than the pit, and I did not care to strike a match. I felt my way along by the wall till I came to a door on the left; it was locked. A little further was another door, also locked. I listened intently, for I fancied I could hear a faint murmur of voices, but I was not sure. Then I startled myself by stepping on nothing—I was at the head of a flight of stone steps; down below I could distinguish an almost imperceptible glimmer of light.

"I'm in for it. Here goes!" I reflected, and I crept down the steps one by one, and in due course reached the bottom. To the left was a doorway, through which came the glimmer of light. Passing through the doorway,

I came into a room with a stone floor. The light, which was no stronger than the very earliest intimation of a winter's dawn, seemed to issue in a most unusual way from the far corner of this apartment near the ceiling. I directed my course towards it, and in the transit made violent contact with some metallic object, which proved to be an upright iron shaft, perhaps three inches in diameter, running from floor to ceiling.

"Surely," I thought, "this is the queerest room I was ever in."

Circumnavigating the pillar, I reached the desired corner, and stood under the feeble source of light. I could see now that in this corner the ceiling was higher than elsewhere, and that the light shone dimly from a perpendicular pane of glass which joined the two levels of the ceiling. I also saw that there was a ledge about two feet from the floor, upon which a man would stand in order to look through the pane.

I climbed on to the ledge, and I looked. To my astonishment, I had a full view of a large apartment, my head being even with the floor of that apartment. Lying on a couch was a woman—the woman who had accosted me on Dover Pier—Carlotta Deschamps, in fact. By her side, facing her in a chair, was Rosetta Rosa. I could hear nothing, but by the movement of their lips I knew that these two were talking. Rosa's face was full of pity; as for Deschamps, her coarse features were inscrutable. She had a certain pallor, but it was impossible to judge whether she was ill or well.

I had scarcely begun to observe the two women when I caught the sound of footsteps on the stone stair. The footsteps approached; they entered the room where I was. I made no sound. Without any hesitation the footsteps arrived at my corner, and a pair of hands touched my legs. Then I knew it was time to act. Jumping down from the ledge, I clasped the intruder by the head, and we rolled over together, struggling. But he was a short man, apparently stiff in the limbs, and in ten seconds or thereabouts I had him flat on his back, and my hand at his throat.

"Don't move," I advised him.

In that faint light I could not see him, so I struck a match, and held it over the man's face. We gazed at each other, breathing heavily.

"Good God!" the man exclaimed.

It was Sir Cyril Smart.

XV

THE SHEATH OF THE DAGGER

THAT WAS ONE OF THOSE supremely trying moments which occur, I suppose, once or twice in the lives of most men, when events demand to be fully explained while time will on no account permit of the explanation. I felt that I must know at once the reason and purpose of Sir Cyril's presence with me in the underground chamber, and that I could do nothing further until I had such knowledge. And yet I also felt that explanations must inevitably wait until the scene enacting above us was over. I stood for a second silent, irresolute. The match went out.

"Are you here to protect her?" whispered Sir Cyril.

"Yes, if she is in danger. I will tell you afterwards about things. And you?"

"I was passing through Paris, and I heard that Deschamps was threatening Rosa. Everyone is talking of it, and I heard of the scene at the rehearsal, and I began to guess ... I know Deschamps well. I was afraid for Rosa. Then this morning I met Yvette, Rosa's maid—she's an old acquaintance of mine—and she told me everything. I have many friends in Paris, and I learnt to-night that Deschamps had sent for Rosa. So I have come up to interfere. They are upstairs, are they not? Let us watch."

"You know the house, then?"

"I have been here before, to one of Deschamps' celebrated suppers. She showed me all over it then. It is one of the strangest houses round about Paris—and that's saying something. The inside was rebuilt by a Russian count who wanted to do the Louis Quinze revelry business over again. He died, and Deschamps bought the place. She often stays here quite alone."

I was putting all the questions. Sir Cyril seemed not to be very curious concerning the origin of my presence.

"What is Rosa to you?" I queried with emphasis.

"What is she to you?" he returned quickly.

"To me she is everything," I said.

"And to me, my young friend!"

I could not, of course, see Sir Cyril's face, but the tone of his reply impressed and silenced me. I was mystified—and yet I felt glad that he was there. Both of us forgot to be surprised at the peculiarity of the scene. It appeared quite natural that he should have supervened so dramatically at precisely the correct moment, and I asked him for no more information. He evidently did know the place, for he crept immediately to the ledge, and looked into the room above. I followed, and stood by his side. The two women were still talking.

"Can't we get into the room, or do something?" I murmured.

"Not yet. How do we know that Deschamps means harm? Let us wait. Have you a weapon?"

Sir Cyril spoke as one in command, and I accepted the assumption of authority.

"Yes," I said; "I've got a revolver, and a little dagger."

"Who knows what may happen? Give me one of them—give me the dagger, if you like."

I passed it to him in the darkness. Astounding as it may seem, I am prepared solemnly to assert that at that moment I had forgotten the history of the dagger, and Sir Cyril's connection with it.

I was just going to ask of what use weapons could be, situated as we were, when I saw Deschamps with a sudden movement jump up from her bed, her eyes blazing. With an involuntary cry in my throat I hammered the glass in front of us with the butt of my revolver, but it was at least an inch thick, and did not even splinter. Sir Cyril sprang from the ledge instantly. Meanwhile Rosa, the change of whose features showed that she divined the shameful trick played upon her, stood up, half-indignant, half-terrified. Deschamps was no more dying than I was; her eyes burned with the lust of homicide, and with uplifted twitching hands she advanced like a tiger, and Rosa retreated before her to the middle of the room.

Then there was the click of a spring, and a square of the centre of the floor, with Rosa standing upon it, swiftly descended into the room where we were. The thing was as startling as a stage illusion; yes, a thousand-fold more startling than any trick I ever saw. I may state here, what I learnt afterwards, that the room above was originally a dining-room, and the arrangement of the trap had been designed to cause a table to disappear and reappear as tables were wont to do at the notorious banquets of King Louis in the Petit Trianon. The glass observatory enabled the kitchen attendants to watch the progress of the meals. Sir Cyril knew of the contrivance, and, rushing to the upright pillar, had worked it most opportunely.

The kitchen, as I may now call it, was illuminated with light from the room above. I hastened to Rosa, who on seeing Sir Cyril and myself gave a little cry, and fell forward fainting. She was a brave girl, but one may have too many astonishments. I caught her, and laid her gently on the floor. Meanwhile Deschamps (the dying Deschamps!) stood on the edge of the upper floor, stamping and shouting in a high fever of foiled revenge. She was mad. When I say that she was mad, I mean that she was merely and simply insane. I could perceive it instantly, and I foresaw that we should have trouble with her.

Without the slightest warning, she jumped down into the midst of us. The distance was a good ten feet, but with a lunatic's luck she did not hurt herself. She faced Sir Cyril, shaking in every limb with passion, and he, calm, determined, unhurried, raised his dagger to defend himself against this terrible lioness should the need arise.

But as he lifted the weapon his eye fell on it; he saw what it was; he had not observed it before, since we had been in darkness. And as he looked his composure seemed to desert him. He paled, and his hand trembled

and hung loosely. The mad woman, seizing her chance, snatched the
dagger from him, and like a flash of lightning drove it into his left breast.
Sir Cyril sank down, the dagger sticking out from his light overcoat.

The deed was over before I could move. I sprang forward. Deschamps
laughed, and turned to me. I closed with her. She scratched and bit, and
she was by no means a weak woman. At first I feared that in her fury
she would overpower me. At length, however, I managed to master her;
but her strength was far from exhausted, and she would not yield. She
was mad; time was passing. I could not afford to be nice in my methods,
so I contrived to stun her, and proceeded to tie her hands with my
handkerchief. Then, panting, I stood up to survey the floor.

I may be forgiven, perhaps, if at that frightful crisis I was not perfectly
cool, and could not decide on the instant upon the wisest course of
action to pursue. Sir Cyril was insensible, and a little circle of blood was
forming round the dagger; Deschamps was insensible, with a dark bruise
on her forehead, inflicted during our struggle; Rosa was insensible—I
presumed from excess of emotion at the sudden fright.

I gazed at the three prone forms, pondering over my handiwork
and that of Chance. What should be the next step? Save for my own
breathing, there was a deathlike silence. The light from the empty room
above rained down upon us through the trap, illuminating the still faces
with its yellow glare. Was any other person in the house? From what
Sir Cyril had said, and from my own surmises, I thought not. Whatever
people Deschamps might have employed to carry messages, she had
doubtless dismissed them. She and Rosa had been alone in the building.
I can understand now that there was something peculiarly attractive
to the diseased imagination of Deschamps in the prospect of inviting
her victim to the snare, and working vengeance upon a rival unaided,
unseen, solitary in that echoing and deserted mansion. I was horribly
perplexed. It struck me that I ought to be gloomily sorrowful, but I was
not. At the bottom of my soul I felt happy, for Rosa was saved.

It was Rosa who first recovered consciousness, and her movement
in sitting up recalled me to my duty. I ran to Sir Cyril, and, kneeling
down so as to screen his body from her sight, I drew the dagger from

its sheath, and began hastily, with such implements as I could contrive on the spur of the moment, to attend to his wound.

"What has happened?" Rosa inquired feebly.

I considered my reply, and then, without turning towards her, I spoke in a slow, matter-of-fact voice.

"Listen carefully to what I say. There has been a plot to—to do you injury. But you are not hurt. You are, in fact, quite well—don't imagine anything else. Sir Cyril Smart is here; he's hurt; Deschamps has wounded him. Deschamps is harmless for the moment, but she may recover and break out again. So I can't leave to get help. You must go. You have fainted, but I am sure you can walk quite well. Go up the stairs here, and walk along the hall till you come to the front door; it is not fastened. Go out into the street, and bring back two gendarmes—two, mind—and a cab, if you can. Do you understand?"

"Yes, but how—"

"Now, please go at once!" I insisted grimly and coldly. "We can talk afterwards. Just do as you're told."

Cowed by the roughness of my tone, she rose and went. I heard her light, hesitating step pass through the hall, and so out of the house.

In a few minutes I had done all that could be done for Sir Cyril, as he lay there. The wound was deep, having regard to the small size of the dagger, and I could only partially stop the extravasation of blood, which was profuse. I doubted if he would recover. It was not long, however, before he regained his senses. He spoke, and I remember vividly now how pathetic to me was the wagging of his short grey beard as his jaw moved.

"Foster," he said—"your name is Foster, isn't it? Where did you find that dagger?"

"You must keep quiet," I said. "I have sent for assistance."

"Don't be a fool, man. You know I'm done for. Tell me how you got the dagger."

So I told him.

"Ah!" he murmured. "It's my luck!" he sighed. Then in little detached sentences, with many pauses, he began to relate a history of what happened after Rosa and I had left him on the night of Sullivan's reception. Much of it was incomprehensible to me; sometimes I could not make out the words. But it seemed that he had followed us in his carriage, had somehow met Rosa again, and then, in a sudden frenzy of remorse, had attempted to kill himself with the dagger in the street. His reason for this I did not gather. His coachman and footman had taken him home, and the affair had been kept quiet.

Remorse for what? I burned to ask a hundred questions, but, fearing to excite him, I shut my lips.

"You are in love with her?" he asked.

I nodded. It was a reply as abrupt as his demand. At that moment Deschamps laughed quietly behind me. I turned round quickly, but she lay still; though she had come to, the fire in her eyes was quenched, and I anticipated no immediate difficulty with her.

"I knew that night that you were in love with her," Sir Cyril continued. "Has she told you about—about me?"

"No," I said.

"I have done her a wrong, Foster—her and another. But she will tell you. I can't talk now. I'm going—going. Tell her that I died in trying to protect her; say that—Foster—say—" He relapsed into unconsciousness.

I heard firm, rapid steps in the hall, and in another instant the representatives of French law had taken charge of the house. Rosa followed them in. She looked wistfully at Sir Cyril, and then, flinging herself down by his side, burst into wild tears.

XVI

THE THING IN THE CHAIR

O**N THE FOLLOWING NIGHT** I sat once more in the salon of Rosa's
flat. She had had Sir Cyril removed thither. He was dying; I had
done my best, but his case was quite hopeless, and at Rosa's urgent
entreaty I had at last left her alone by his bedside.

I need not recount all the rush of incidents that had happened
since the tragedy at the Villa des Hortensias on the previous evening.
Most people will remember the tremendous sensation caused by the
judicial inquiry—an inquiry which ended in the tragical Deschamps
being incarcerated in the Charenton Asylum. For aught I know, the
poor woman, once one of the foremost figures in the gaudy world of
theatrical Paris, is still there consuming her heart with a futile hate.

Rosa would never refer in any way to the interview between
Deschamps and herself; it was as if she had hidden the memory of
it in some secret chamber of her soul, which nothing could induce
her to open again. But there can be no doubt that Deschamps had
intended to murder her, and, indeed, would have murdered her had
it not been for the marvellously opportune arrival of Sir Cyril. With
the door of the room locked as it was, I should assuredly have been
condemned, lacking Sir Cyril's special knowledge of the house, to the
anguish of witnessing a frightful crime without being able to succour
the victim. To this day I can scarcely think of that possibility and remain
calm.

As for Sir Cyril's dramatic appearance in the villa, when I had learnt all the facts, that was perhaps less extraordinary than it had seemed to me from our hasty dialogue in the underground kitchen of Deschamps' house. Although neither Rosa nor I was aware of it, operatic circles had been full of gossip concerning Deschamps' anger and jealousy, of which she made no secret. One or two artists of the Opéra Comique had decided to interfere, or at any rate seriously to warn Rosa, when Sir Cyril arrived, on his way to London from the German watering-place where he had been staying. All Paris knew Sir Cyril, and Sir Cyril knew all Paris; he was made acquainted with the facts directly, and the matter was left to him. A man of singular resolution, originality, and courage, he had gone straight to the Rue Thiers, having caught a rumour, doubtless started by the indiscreet Deschamps herself, that Rosa would be decoyed there. The rest was mere good fortune.

In regard to the mysterious connection between Sir Cyril and Rosa, I had at present no clue to it; nor had there been much opportunity for conversation between Rosa and myself. We had not even spoken to each other alone, and, moreover, I was uncertain whether she would care to enlighten me on that particular matter; assuredly I had no right to ask her to do so. Further, I was far more interested in another, and to me vastly more important, question, the question of Lord Clarenceux and his supposed death.

I was gloomily meditating upon the tangle of events, when the door of the salon opened, and Rosa entered. She walked stiffly to a chair, and, sitting down opposite to me, looked into my face with hard, glittering eyes. For a few moments she did not speak, and I could not break the silence. Then I saw the tears slowly welling up, and I was glad for that. She was intensely moved, and less agonizing experiences than she had gone through might easily have led to brain fever in a woman of her highly emotional temperament.

"Why don't you leave me, Mr Foster?" she cried passionately, and there were sobs in her voice. "Why don't you leave me, and never see me again?"

"Leave you?" I said softly. "Why?"

"Because I am cursed. Throughout my life I have been cursed; and the curse clings, and it falls on those who come near me."

She gave way to hysterical tears; her head bent till it was almost on her knees. I went to her, and gently raised it, and put a cushion at the back of the chair. She grew calmer.

"If you are cursed, I will be cursed," I said, gazing straight at her, and then I sat down again.

The sobbing gradually ceased. She dried her eyes.

"He is dead," she said shortly.

I made no response; I had none to make.

"You do not say anything," she murmured.

"I am sorry. Sir Cyril was the right sort."

"He was my father," she said.

"Your father!" I repeated. No revelation could have more profoundly astonished me.

"Yes," she firmly repeated.

We both paused.

"I thought you had lost both parents," I said at length, rather lamely.

"Till lately I thought so too. Listen. I will tell you the tale of all my life. Not until to-night have I been able to put it together, and fill in the blanks."

And this is what she told me:

"My father was travelling through Europe. He had money, and of course he met with adventures. One of his adventures was my mother. She lived among the vines near Avignon, in Southern France; her uncle was a small grape-grower. She belonged absolutely to the people, but she was extremely beautiful. I'm not exaggerating; she was. She was one of those women that believe everything, and my father fell in love with her. He married her properly at Avignon. They travelled together through France and Italy, and then to Belgium. Then, in something less than a year, I was born. She gave herself up to me entirely. She was not clever; she had no social talents and no ambitions. No, she certainly had not much brain; but to balance that she had a heart—so large that it completely enveloped my father and me.

"After three years he had had enough of my mother. He got restive. He was ambitious. He wanted to shine in London, where he was known, and where his family had made traditions in the theatrical world. But he felt that my mother wouldn't—wouldn't be suitable for London. Fancy the absurdity of a man trying to make a name in London when hampered by a wife who was practically of the peasant class! He simply left her. Oh, it was no common case of desertion. He used his influence over my mother to make her consent. She did consent. It broke her heart, but hers was the sort of love that suffers, so she let him go. He arranged to allow her a reasonable income.

"I can just remember a man who must have been my father. I was three years old when he left us. Till then we had lived in a large house in an old city. Can't you guess what house that was? Of course you can. Yes, it was the house at Bruges where Alresca died. We gave up that house, my mother and I, and went to live in Italy. Then my father sold the house to Alresca. I only knew that to-day. You may guess my childish recollections of Bruges aren't very distinct. It was part of the understanding that my mother should change her name, and at Pisa she was known as Madame Montigny. That was the only surname of hers that I ever knew.

"As I grew older, my mother told me fairy-tales to account for the absence of my father. She died when I was sixteen, and before she died she told me the truth. She begged me to promise to go to him, and said that I should be happy with him. But I would not promise. I was sixteen then, and very proud. What my mother had told me made me hate and despise my father. I left my dead mother's side hating him; I had a loathing for him which words couldn't express. She had omitted to tell me his real name; I never asked her, and I was glad not to know it. In speaking of him, of course she always said 'your father', 'your father', and she died before she got quite to the end of her story. I buried my mother, and then I was determined to disappear. My father might search, but he should never find me. The thought that he would search and search, and be unhappy for the rest of his life because he couldn't find me, gave me a kind of joy. So I left Pisa, and I took with me nothing but the few hundred lire which my mother had by her, and the toy dagger—my father's gift—which she had always worn in her hair.

"I knew that I had a voice. Everyone said that, and my mother had had it trained up to a certain point. I knew that I could make a reputation. I adopted the name of Rosetta Rosa, and I set to work. Others have suffered worse things than I suffered. I made my way. Sir Cyril Smart, the great English impresario, heard me at Genoa, and offered me an engagement in London. Then my fortune was made. You know that story—everyone knows it.

"Why did I not guess at once that he was my father? I cannot tell. And not having guessed it at once, why should I ever have guessed it? I cannot tell. The suspicion stole over me gradually. Let me say that I always was conscious of a peculiar feeling towards Sir Cyril Smart, partly antagonistic, yet not wholly so—a feeling I could never understand. Then suddenly I knew, beyond any shadow of doubt, that Sir Cyril was my father, and in the same moment he knew that I was his daughter. You were there; you saw us in the portico of the reception-rooms at that London hotel. I caught him staring at the dagger in my hair just as if he was staring at a snake—I had not worn it for some time—and the knowledge of his identity swept over me like a—like a big wave. I hated him more than ever.

"That night, it seems, he followed us in his carriage to Alresca's flat. When I came out of the flat he was waiting. He spoke. I won't tell you what he said, and I won't tell you what I said. But I was very curt and very cruel." Her voice trembled. "I got into my carriage. My God! how cruel I was! To-night he—my father—has told me that he tried to kill himself with my mother's dagger, there on the pavement. I had driven him to suicide."

She stopped. "Do you blame me?" she murmured.

"I do not blame you," I said. "But he is dead, and death ends all things."

"You are right," she said. "And he loved me at the last. I know that. And he saved my life—you and he. He has atoned—atoned for his conduct to my poor mother. He died with my kiss on his lips."

And now the tears came into my eyes.

"Ah!" she exclaimed, and the pathos of her ringing tones was intolerable to me. "You may well weep for me." Then with abrupt change she laughed. "Don't you agree that I am cursed? Am I not cursed? Say it! say it!"

"I will not say it," I answered. "Why should you be cursed? What do you mean?"

"I do not know what I mean, but I know what I feel. Look back at my life. My mother died, deserted. My father has died, killed by a mad woman. My dear friend Alresca died—who knows how? Clarenceux—he too died."

"Stay!" I almost shouted, springing up, and the suddenness of my excitement intimidated her. "How do you know that Lord Clarenceux is dead?"

I stood before her, trembling with apprehension for the effect of the disclosure I was about to make. She was puzzled and alarmed by the violent change in me, but she controlled herself.

"How do I know?" she repeated with strange mildness.

"Yes, how do you know? Did you see him die?"

I had a wild desire to glance over my shoulder at the portrait.

"No, my friend. But I saw him after he was dead. He died suddenly in Vienna. Don't let us talk about that."

"Aha!" I laughed incredulously, and then, swiftly driven forward by an overpowering impulse, I dropped on my knees and seized her hands with a convulsive grasp. "Rosa! Rosa!"—my voice nearly broke—"you must know that I love you. Say that you love me—that you would love me whether Clarenceux were dead or alive."

An infinite tenderness shone in her face. She put out her hand, and to calm me stroked my hair.

"Carl!" she whispered.

It was enough. I got up. I did not kiss her.

A servant entered, and said that someone from the theatre had called to see mademoiselle on urgent business. Excusing herself, Rosa went out. I held open the door for her, and closed it slowly with a sigh of incredible relief. Then I turned back into the room. I was content to be alone for a little while.

Great God! The chair which Rosa had but that instant left was not empty. Occupying it was a figure—the figure of the man whose portrait hung on the wall—the figure of the man who had haunted me ever since I met Rosa—the figure of Lord Clarenceux, whom Rosa had seen dead.

At last, oh, powers of hell, I knew you! The inmost mystery stood clear. In one blinding flash of comprehension I felt the fullness of my calamity. This man that I had seen was not a man, but a malign and jealous spirit—using his spectral influences to crush the mortals bold enough to love the woman whom he had loved on earth. The death of Alresca, the unaccountable appearances in the cathedral, in the train, on the steamer—everything was explained. And before that coldly sneering, triumphant face, which bore the look of life, and which I yet knew to be impalpable, I shook with the terrified ague of a culprit.

A minute or a thousand years might have passed. Then Rosa returned. In an instant the apparition had vanished. But by her pallid, drawn face and her grey lips I knew that she had seen it. Truly she was cursed, and I with her!

XVII
THE MENACE

FROM THE MOMENT OF MY avowal to Rosa it seemed that the evil spirit of the dead Lord Clarenceux had assumed an ineffable dominion over me. I cannot properly describe it; I cannot describe it all. I may only say that I felt I had suddenly become the subject of a tyrant who would punish me if I persisted in any course of conduct to which he objected. I knew what fear was—the most terrible of all fears—the fear of that which we cannot understand. The inmost and central throne of my soul was commanded by this implacable ghost, this ghost which did not speak, but which conveyed its ideas by means of a single glance, a single sneer.

It was strange that I should be aware at once what was required of me, and the reasons for these requirements. Till that night I had never guessed the nature of the thing which for so many weeks had been warning me; I had not even guessed that I was being warned; I had taken for a man that which was not a man. Yet now, in an instant of time, all was clear down to the smallest details. From the primal hour when a liking for Rosa had arisen in my breast, the ghost of Lord Clarenceux, always hovering uneasily near to its former love, had showed itself to me.

The figure opposite the Devonshire Mansion—that was the first warning. With regard to the second appearance, in the cathedral of Bruges, I surmised that that only indirectly affected myself. Primarily it was the celebration of a fiendish triumph over one who had preceded me in daring to love Rosetta Rosa, but doubtless also it was meant in a subsidiary degree as a second warning to the youth who followed in Alresca's footsteps. Then there were the two appearances during my journey from London to Paris with Rosa's jewels—in the train and on the steamer. Matters by that time had become more serious. I was genuinely in love, and the ghost's anger was quickened. The train was wrecked and the steamer might have been sunk, and I could not help thinking that the ghost, in some ineffectual way, had been instrumental in both these disasters. The engine-driver, who said he was "dazed," and the steersman, who attributed his mistake at the wheel to the interference of some unknown outsider—were not these things an indication that my dreadful suspicion was well grounded? And if so, to what frightful malignity did they not point! Here was a spirit, which in order to appease the pangs of a supernatural jealousy, was ready to use its immaterial powers to destroy scores of people against whom it could not possibly have any grudge. The most fanatical anarchism is not worse than this.

Those attempts had failed. But now the aspect of affairs was changed. The ghost of Lord Clarenceux had more power over me now—I felt that acutely; and I explained it by the fact that I was in the near neighbourhood of Rosa. It was only when she was near that the jealous hate of this spectre exercised its full efficacy.

In such wise did I reason the matter out to myself. But reasoning was quite unnecessary. I knew by a sure instinct. All the dark thoughts of the ghost had passed into my brain, and if they had been transcribed in words of fire and burnt upon my retina, I could not have been more certain of their exact import.

As I sat in my room at the hotel that night I speculated morosely upon my plight and upon the future. Had a man ever been so situated before? Well, probably so. We go about in a world where secret influences are continually at work for us or against us, and we do not suspect their existence, because we have no imagination. For it needs imagination to perceive the truth—that is why the greatest poets are always the greatest teachers.

As for you who are disposed to smile at the idea of a live man crushed (figuratively) under the heel of a ghost, I beg you to look back upon your own experience, and count up the happenings which have struck you as mysterious. You will be astonished at their number. But nothing is so mysterious that it is incapable of explanation, did we but know enough. I, by a singular mischance, was put in the way of the nameless knowledge which explains all. At any rate, I was made acquainted with some trifle of it. I had strayed on the seashore of the unknown, and picked up a pebble. I had a glimpse of that other world which permeates and exists side by side with and permeates our own.

Just now I used the phrase 'under the heel of a ghost,' and I used it advisedly. It indicates pretty well my mental condition. I was cowed, mastered. The ghost of Clarenceux, driven to extremities by the brief scene of tenderness which had passed in Rosa's drawing-room, had determined by his own fell method to end the relations between Rosa and myself. And his method was to assume a complete sway over me, the object of his hatred.

How did he exercise that sway? Can I answer? I cannot. How does one man influence another? Not by electric wires or chemical apparatus, but by those secret channels through which intelligence meets intelligence. All I know is that I felt his sinister authority. During life Clarenceux, according to every account, had been masterful, imperious, commanding; and he carried these attributes with him beyond the grave. His was a stronger personality than mine, and I could not hide from myself the assurance that in the struggle of will against will I should not be the conqueror.

Not that anything had occurred, even the smallest thing! Upon perceiving Rosa the apparition, as I have said, vanished. We did not say much to each other, Rosa and I; we could not—we were afraid. I went to my hotel; I sat in my room alone; I saw no ghost. But I was aware, I was aware of the doom which impended over me. And already, indeed, I experienced the curious sensation of the ebbing of volitional power; I thought even that I was losing my interest in life. My sensations were dulled. It began to appear to me unimportant whether I lived or died. Only I knew that in either case I should love Rosa. My love was independent of my will, and therefore the ghost of Clarenceux, do what it might, could not tear it from me. I might die, I might suffer mental tortures inconceivable, but I should continue to love. In this idea lay my only consolation.

I remained motionless in my chair for hours, and then—it was soon after the clocks struck four—I sprang up, and searched among my papers for Alresca's letter, the seal of which, according to his desire, was still intact. The letter had been in my mind for a long time. I knew well that the moment for opening it had come, that the circumstances to which Alresca had referred in his covering letter had veritably happened. But somehow, till that instant, I had not been able to find courage to read the communication. As I opened it I glanced out of the window. The first sign of dawn was in the sky. I felt a little easier.

Here is what I read:

My dear Carl Foster,

When you read this the words I am about to write will have acquired the sanction which belongs to the utterances of those who have passed away. Give them, therefore, the most serious consideration.

If you are not already in love with Rosetta Rosa you soon will be. I, too, as you know, have loved her. Let me tell you some of the things which happened to me.

From the moment when that love first sprang up in my heart I began to be haunted by—I will not say what; you know without being told, for whoever loves Rosa will be haunted as I was, as I am. Rosa has been loved once for all, and with a passion so intense that it has survived the grave. For months I disregarded the visitations, relying on the strength of my own soul. I misjudged myself, or, rather, I underestimated my adversary—the great man who in life had loved Rosa. I proposed to Rosa, and she refused me. But that did not quench my love. My love grew; I encouraged it; and it was against the mere fact of my love that the warnings were directed.

You remember the accident on the stage which led to our meeting. That accident was caused by sheer terror—the terror of an apparition more awful than any that had gone before.

Still I persisted—I persisted in my hopeless love. Then followed that unnamed malady which in vain you are seeking to cure, a malady which was accompanied by innumerable and terrifying phenomena. The malady was one of the mind; it robbed me of the desire to live. More than that, it made life intolerable. At last I surrendered. I believe I am a brave man, but it is the privilege of the brave man to surrender without losing honour to an adversary who has proved his superiority. Yes, I surrendered. I cast out love in order that I might live for my art.

"But I was too late. I had pushed too far the enmity of this spectral and unrelenting foe, and it would not accept my surrender. I have dashed the image of Rosa from my heart, and I have done it to no purpose. I am dying. And so I write this for you, lest you should go unwarned to the same doom.

The love of Rosa is worth dying for, if you can win it. (I could not even win it.) You will have to choose between Love and Life. I do not counsel you either way. But I urge you to choose. I urge you either to defy your foe utterly and to the death, or to submit before submission is useless.

Alresca

I sat staring at the paper long after I had finished reading it, thinking about poor Alresca. There was a date to it, and this date showed that it was written a few days before his mysterious disease took a turn for the better.

The communication accordingly needs some explanation. It seems to me that Alresca was mistaken. His foe was not so implacable as Alresca imagined. Alresca having surrendered in the struggle between them, the ghost of Lord Clarenceux hesitated, and then ultimately withdrew its hateful influence, and Alresca recovered. Then Rosa came again into his existence that evening at Bruges. Alresca, scornful of consequences, let his passion burst once more into flame, and the ghost instantly, in a flash of anger, worked its retribution.

Day came, and during the whole of that day I pondered upon a phrase in Alresca's letter, "You will have to choose between love and life." But I could not choose. Love is the greatest thing in life; one may, however, question whether it should be counted greater than life itself. I tried to argue the question calmly, dispassionately. As if such questions may be argued! I could not give up my love; I could not give up my life; that was how all my calm, dispassionate arguments ended. At one moment I was repeating, "The love of Rosa is worth dying for;" at the next I was busy with the high and dear ambitions of which I had so often dreamed. Were these to be sacrificed? Moreover, what use would Rosa's love be to me when I was dead? And what use would my life be to me without my love for her?

A hundred times I tried to laugh, and said to myself that I was the victim of fancy, that I should see nothing further of this prodigious apparition; that, in short, my brain had been overtaxed by recent events, and I had suffered from delusions. Vain and conventional self-deceptions! At the bottom of my soul lay always the secret and profound conviction that I was doomed, cursed, caught in the toils of a relentless foe who was armed with all the strange terrors of the unknown; a foe whose onslaughts it was absolutely impossible for me to parry.

As the hours passed a yearning to see Rosa, to be near her, came upon me. I fought against it, fearing I know not what as the immediate consequence. I wished to temporize, or, at any rate, to decide upon a definite course of conduct before I saw her again. But towards evening I felt that I should yield to the impulse to behold her. I said to myself, as though I needed some excuse, that she would have a great deal of trouble with the arrangements for Sir Cyril's funeral, and that I ought to offer my assistance; that, indeed, I ought to have offered my assistance early in the day.

I presented myself after dinner. She was dressed in black, and her manner was nervous, flurried, ill at ease. We shook hands very formally, and then could find nothing to say to each other. Had she, with a woman's instinct, guessed, from that instant's view of the thing in the chair last night, all that was involved for me in our love? If not all, she had guessed most of it. She had guessed that the powerful spirit of Lord Clarenceux was inimical, fatally inimical, to me. None knew better than herself the terrible strength of his jealousy. I wondered what were her thoughts, her secret desires.

At length she began to speak of commonplace matters.

"Guess who has called," she said, with a little smile.

"I give it up," I said, with a smile as artificial as her own.

"Mrs Sullivan Smith. She and Sullivan Smith are on their way home from Bayreuth; they are at the Hôtel du Rhin. She wanted to know all about what happened in the Rue Thiers, and to save trouble I told her. She stayed a long time. There have been a lot of callers. I am very tired. I—I expected you earlier. But you are not listening."

I was not. I was debating whether or not to show her Alresca's letter. I decided to do so, and I handed it to her there and then.

"Read that," I murmured.

She read it in silence, and then looked at me. Her tender eyes were filled with tears. I cast away all my resolutions of prudence, of wariness, before that gaze. Seizing her in my arms, I kissed her again and again.

"I have always suspected—what—what Alresca says," she murmured.

"But you love me?" I cried passionately.

"Do you need to be told, my poor Carl?" she replied, with the most exquisite melancholy.

"Then I'll defy hell itself!" I said.

She hung passive in my embrace.

XVIII

THE STRUGGLE

WHEN I GOT BACK TO my little sitting-room at the Hôtel de
Portugal, I experienced a certain timid hesitation in opening the
door. For several seconds I stood before it, the key in the lock, afraid
to enter. I wanted to rush out again, to walk the streets all night; it was
raining, but I thought that anything would be preferable to the inside of
my sitting-room. Then I felt that, whatever the cost, I must go in; and,
twisting the key, I pushed heavily at the door, and entered, touching as I
did so the electric switch. In the chair which stood before the writing-
table in the middle of the room sat the figure of Lord Clarenceux.

Yes, my tormentor was indeed waiting. I had defied him, and we were
about to try a fall. As for me, I may say that my heart sank, sick with an
ineffable fear. The figure did not move as I went in; its back was towards
me. At the other end of the room was the doorway which led to the
small bedroom, little more than an alcove, and the gaze of the apparition
was fixed on this doorway.

I closed the outer door behind me, and locked it, and then I stood still.
In the looking-glass over the mantelpiece I saw a drawn, pale, agitated face
in which all the trouble of the world seemed to reside; it was my own face.
I was alone in the room with the ghost—the ghost which, jealous of my
love for the woman it had loved, meant to revenge itself by my death.

A ghost, did I say? To look at it, no one would have taken it for
an apparition. No wonder that till the previous evening I had never

suspected it to be other than a man. It was dressed in black; it had the very aspect of life. I could follow the creases in the frock coat, the direction of the nap of the silk hat which it wore in my room. How well by this time I knew that faultless black coat and that impeccable hat! Yet it seemed that I could not examine them too closely. I pierced them with the intensity of my fascinated glance. Yes, I pierced them, for showing faintly through the coat I could discern the outline of the table which should have been hidden by the man's figure, and through the hat I could see the handle of the French window.

As I stood motionless there, solitary under the glow of the electric light with this fearful visitor, I began to wish that it would move. I wanted to face it—to meet its gaze with my gaze, eye to eye, and will against will. The battle between us must start at once, I thought, if I was to have any chance of victory, for moment by moment I could feel my resolution, my manliness, my mere physical courage, slipping away.

But the apparition did not stir. Impassive, remorseless, sinister, it was content to wait, well aware that all suspense was in its favour. Then I said to myself that I would cross the room, and so attain my object. I made a step—and drew back, frightened by the sound of a creaking board. Absurd! But it was quite a minute before I dared to make another step. I had meant to walk straight across to the other door, passing in my course close by the occupied chair. I did not do so; I kept round by the wall, creeping on tiptoe and my eye never leaving the figure in the chair. I did this in spite of myself, and the manner of my action was the first hint of an ultimate defeat.

At length I stood in the doorway leading to the bedroom. I could feel the perspiration on my forehead and at the back of my neck. I fronted the inscrutable white face of the thing which had once been Lord Clarenceux, the lover of Rosetta Rosa; I met its awful eyes, dark, invidious, fateful. Ah, those eyes! Even in my terror I could read in them all the history, all the characteristics, of Lord Clarenceux. They were the eyes of one capable at once of the highest and of the lowest. Mingled with their hardness was a melting softness, with their cruelty a large benevolence, with their hate a pitying tenderness, with their spirituality a hellish turpitude. They were the eyes of two opposite men, and as I gazed into them they reconciled for me the conflicting accounts of Lord Clarenceux which I had heard from different people.

But as far as I was concerned that night the eyes held nothing but cruelty and disaster; though I could detect in them the other qualities, those qualities were not for me. We faced each other, the apparition and I, and the struggle, silent and bitter as the grave, began. Neither of us moved. My arms were folded easily, but my nails pressed in the palms of my clenched hands. My teeth were set, my lips tight together, my glance unswerving. By sheer strength of endeavour I cast aside all my forebodings of defeat, and in my heart I said with the profoundest conviction that I would love Rosa though the seven seas and all the continents gave up their dead to frighten me.

So we remained, for how long I do not know. It may have been hours; it may have been only minutes; I cannot tell. Then gradually there came over me a feeling that the ghost in the chair was growing larger. The ghastly inhuman sneer on his thin widening lips assaulted me like a giant's malediction. And the light in the room seemed to become more brilliant, till it was almost blinding with the dazzle of its whiteness. This went on for a time, and once more I pulled myself together, collected my scattering senses, and seized again the courage and determination which had nearly slipped from me.

But I knew that I must get away, out of sight of this moveless and diabolic figure, which did not speak, but which made known its commands by means of its eyes alone. "Resign her!" the eyes said. "Tear your love for her out of your heart! Swear that you will never see her again—or I will ruin you utterly, not only now, but for evermore!"

And though I trembled, my eyes answered "No."

For some reason which I cannot at all explain, I suddenly took off my overcoat, and, drawing aside the screen which ran across the corner of the room at my right hand, forming a primitive sort of wardrobe, I hung it on one of the hooks. I had to feel with my fingers for the hook, because I kept my gaze on the figure.

"I will go into the bedroom," I said.

And I half-turned to pass through the doorway. Then I stopped. If I did so, the eyes of the ghost would be upon my back, and I felt that I could only withstand that glance by meeting it. To have it on my back! … Doubtless I was going mad. However, I went backwards through the doorway, and then rapidly stepped out of sight of the apparition, and sat down upon the bed.

Useless! I must return. The mere idea of the empty sitting-room— empty with the ghost in it—filled me with a new and stranger fear. Horrible happenings might occur in that room, and I must be there to see them! Moreover, the ghost's gaze must not fall on nothing; that would be too appalling (without doubt I was mad); its gaze must meet something, otherwise it would travel out into space further and further till it had left all the stars and waggled aimless in the ether: the notion of such a calamity was unbearable. Besides, I was hungry for that gaze; my eyes desired those eyes; if that glance did not press against them, they would burst from my head and roll on the floor, and I should be compelled to go down on my hands and knees and grope in search for them. No, no, I must return to the sitting-room. And I returned.

The gaze met me in the doorway. And now there was something novel in it—an added terror, a more intolerable menace, a silent imprecation so frightful that no human being could suffer it. I sank to the ground, and as I did so I shrieked, but it was an unheard shriek, sounding only within the brain. And in reply to that unheard shriek I heard the unheard voice of the ghost crying, "Yield!"

I would not yield. Crushed, maddened, tortured by a worse than any physical torture, I would not yield. But I wanted to die. I felt that death would be sweet and utterly desirable. And so thinking, I faded into a kind of coma, or rather a state which was just short of coma. I had not lost consciousness, but I was conscious of nothing but the gaze.

"Good-bye, Rosa," I whispered. "I'm beaten, but my love has not been conquered."

The next thing I remembered was the paleness of the dawn at the window. The apparition had vanished for that night, and I was alive. But I knew that I had touched the skirts of death; I knew that after another such night I should die.

The morning chocolate arrived, and by force of habit I consumed it. I felt no interest in any earthly thing; my sole sensation was a dread of the coming night, which all too soon would be upon me. For several hours I sat, pale and nerveless, in my room, despising myself for a weakness and a fear which I could not possibly avoid. I was no longer my own master; I was the slave, the shrinking chattel of a ghost, and the thought of my condition was a degradation unspeakable.

During the afternoon a ray of hope flashed upon me. Mrs Sullivan Smith was at the Hôtel du Rhin, so Rosa had said; I would call on her. I remembered her strange demeanour to me on the occasion of our first meeting, and afterwards at the reception. It seemed clear to me now that she must have known something. Perhaps she might help me.

I found her in a garish apartment too full of Louis Philippe furniture, robed in a crimson tea-gown, and apparently doing nothing whatever. She had the calm quiescence of a Spanish woman. Yet when she saw me her eyes burned with a sudden dark excitement.

"Carl," she said, with the most staggering abruptness, "you are dying."

"How do you know?" I said morosely. "Do I look it?"

"Yet the crystal warned you!" she returned, with apparent but not real inconsequence.

"I want you to tell me," I said eagerly, and with no further pretence. "You must have known something then, when you made me look in the crystal. What did you know—and how?"

She sat a moment in thought, stately, half-languid, mysterious.

"First," she said, "let me hear all that has happened. Then I will tell you."

"Is Sullivan about?" I asked. I felt that if I was to speak I must not be interrupted by that good-natured worldling.

"Sullivan," she said a little scornfully, with gentle contempt, "is learning French billiards. You are perfectly safe." She understood.

Then I told her without the least reservation all that had happened to me, and especially my experiences of the previous night. When I had finished she looked at me with her large sombre eyes, which were full of pity, but not of hope. I waited for her words.

"Now, listen," she said. "You shall hear. I was with Lord Clarenceux when he died."

"You!" I exclaimed. "In Vienna! But even Rosa was not with him. How—"

"Patience! And do not interrupt me with questions. I am giving away a secret which carries with it my—my reputation. Long before my marriage I had known Lord Clarenceux. He knew many women; I was one of them. That affair ended. I married Sullivan.

"I happened to be in Vienna at the time Lord Clarenceux was taken with brain fever. I was performing at a music-hall on the Prater. There was a great rage then for English singers in Vienna. I knew he was alone. I remembered certain things that had passed between us, and I went to him. I helped to nurse him. He was engaged to Rosa, but Rosa was far away, and could not come immediately. He grew worse. The doctors said one day that he must die. That night I was by his bedside. He got suddenly up out of bed. I could not stop him: he had the strength of delirium. He went into his dressing-room, and dressed himself fully, even to his hat, without any assistance.

"'Where are you going?' I said to him.

"'I am going to her,' he said. 'These cursed doctors say I shall die. But I shan't. I want her. Why hasn't she come? I must go and find her.'

"Then he fell across the bed exhausted. He was dying. I had rung for help, but no one had come, and I ran out of the room to call on the landing. When I came back he was sitting up in bed, all dressed, and still with his hat on. It was the last flicker of his strength. His eyes glittered. He began to speak. How he stared at me! I shall never forget it!

"'I am dying!' he said hoarsely. 'They were right, after all. I shall lose her. I would sell my soul to keep her, yet death takes me from her. She is young and beautiful, and will live many years. But I have loved her, and where I have loved let others beware. I shall never be far from her, and if another man should dare to cast eyes on her I will curse him. The heat of my jealousy shall blast his very soul. He, too, shall die. Rosa was mine in life, and she shall be mine in death. My spirit will watch over her, for no man ever loved a woman as I loved Rosa.' Those were his very words, Carl. Soon afterwards he died."

She recited Clarenceux's last phrases with such genuine emotion that I could almost hear Clarenceux himself saying them. I felt sure that she had remembered them precisely, and that Clarenceux would, indeed, have employed just such terms.

"And you believe," I murmured, after a long pause, during which I fitted the remarkable narration in with my experiences, and found that it tallied—"you believe that Lord Clarenceux could keep his word after death?"

"I believe!" she said simply.

"Then there is no hope for me, Emmeline?"

She looked at me vaguely, absently, without speaking, and shook her head. Her lustrous eyes filled with tears.

XIX

THE INTERCESSION

JUST AS I WAS WALKING away from the hotel I perceived Rosa's victoria drawing up before the portico. She saw me. We exchanged a long look—a look charged with anxious questionings. Then she beckoned to me, and I, as it were suddenly waking from a trance, raised my hat, and went to her.

"Get in," she said, without further greeting. "We will drive to the Arc de Triomphe and back. I was going to call on Mrs Sullivan Smith,—just a visit of etiquette,—but I will postpone that."

Her manner was constrained, as it had been on the previous day, but I could see that she was striving hard to be natural. For myself, I did not speak. I felt nervous, even irritable, in my love for her. Gradually, however, her presence soothed me, slackened the tension of my system, and I was able to find a faint pleasure in the beauty of the September afternoon, and of the girl by my side, in the smooth movement of the carriage, and the general gaiety and colour of the broad tree-lined Champs Elysées.

"Why do you ask me to drive with you?" I asked her at length, abruptly yet suavely. Amid the noise of the traffic we could converse with the utmost privacy.

"Because I have something to say to you," she answered, looking straight in front of her.

"Before you say it, one question occurs to me. You are dressed in black; you are in mourning for Sir Cyril, your father, who is not even buried. And yet you told me just now that you were paying a mere visit of etiquette to my cousin Emmeline. Is it usual in Paris for ladies in mourning to go out paying calls? But perhaps you had a special object in calling on Emmeline."

"I had," she replied at once with dignity, "and I did not wish you to know."

"What was it?"

"Really, Mr Foster—"

"'Mr Foster!'"

"Yes; I won't call you Carl any more. I have made a mistake, and it is as well you should hear of it now. I can't love you. I have misunderstood my feelings. What I feel for you is gratitude, not love. I want you to forget me."

She was pale and restless.

"Rosa!" I exclaimed warningly.

"Yes," she continued urgently and feverishly, "forget me. I may seem cruel, but it is best there should be no beating about the bush. I can't love you."

"Rosa!" I repeated.

"Go back to London," she went on. "You have ambitions. Fulfil them. Work at your profession. Above all, don't think of me. And always remember that though I am very grateful to you, I cannot love you—never!"

"That isn't true, Rosa!" I said quietly. "You have invited me into this carriage simply to lie to me. But you are an indifferent liar—it is not your forte. My dear child, do you imagine that I cannot see through your poor little plan? Mrs Sullivan Smith has been talking to you, and it has occurred to you that if you cast me off, the anger of that—that thing may be appeased, and I may be saved from the fate that overtook Alresca. You were calling on Emmeline to ask her advice finally, as she appears to be mixed up in this affair. Then, on seeing me, you decided all of a sudden to take your courage in both hands, and dismiss me at once. It was heroic of you, Rosa; it was a splendid sacrifice of your self-respect. But it can't be. Nothing is going to disturb my love. If I die under some mysterious influence, then I die; but I shall die loving you, and I shall die absolutely certain that you love me."

Her breast heaved, and under the carriage rug her hand found mine and clasped it. We did not look at each other. In a thick voice I called to the coachman to stop. I got out, and the vehicle passed on. If I had stayed with her, I should have wept in sight of the whole street.

I ate no dinner that evening, but spent the hours in wandering up and down the long verdurous alleys in the neighbourhood of the Arc de Triomphe. I was sure of Rosa's love, and that thought gave me a certain invigoration. But to be sure of a woman's love when that love means torture and death to you is not a complete and perfect happiness. No, my heart was full of bitterness and despair, and my mind invaded by a miserable weakness. I pitied myself, and at the same time I scorned myself. After all, the ghost had no actual power over me; a ghost cannot stab, cannot throttle, cannot shoot. A ghost can only act upon the mind, and if the mind is feeble enough to allow itself to be influenced by an intangible illusion, then—

But how futile were such arguments! Whatever the power might be, the fact that the ghost had indeed a power over me was indisputable. All day I had felt the spectral sword of it suspended above my head. My timid footsteps lingering on the way to the hotel sufficiently proved its power. The experiences of the previous night might be merely subjective—conceptions of the imagination—but they were no less real, no less fatal to me on that account.

Once I had an idea of not going to the hotel that night at all. But of what use could such an avoidance be? The apparition was bound by no fetters to that terrible sitting-room of mine. I might be put to the ordeal anywhere, even here in the thoroughfares of the city, and upon the whole I preferred to return to my lodging. Nay, I was the victim of a positive desire for that scene of my torture.

I returned. It was eleven o'clock. The apparition awaited me. But this time it was not seated in the chair. It stood with its back to the window, and its gaze met mine as I entered the room. I did not close the door, and my eyes never left its face. The sneer on its thin lips was bitterer, more devilishly triumphant, than before. Erect, motionless, and inexorable, the ghost stood there, and it seemed to say: "What is the use of leaving the door open? You dare not escape. You cannot keep away from me. To-night you shall die of sheer terror."

With a wild audacity I sat down in the very chair which it had occupied, and drummed my fingers on the writing-table. Then I took off my hat, and with elaborate aim pitched it on to a neighboring sofa. I was making a rare pretence of carelessness. But moment by moment, exactly as before, my courage and resolution oozed out of me, drawn away by that mystic presence.

Once I got up filled with a brilliant notion. I would approach the apparition; I would try to touch it. Could I but do so, it would vanish; I felt convinced it would vanish. I got up, as I say, but I did not approach the ghost. I was unable to move forward, held by a nameless dread. I dropped limply back into the chair. The phenomena of the first night repeated themselves, but more intensely, with a more frightful torture. Once again I sought relief from the agony of that gaze by retreating into the bedroom; once again I was compelled by the same indescribable fear to return, and once again I fell down, smitten by a new and more awful menace, a kind of incredible blasphemy which no human thought can convey.

And now the ghost moved mysteriously and ominously towards me. With an instinct of defence, cowed as I was upon the floor, I raised my hand to ward it off. Useless attempt! It came near and nearer, imperceptibly moving.

"Let me die in peace," I said within my brain.

But it would not. Not only must I die, but in order to die I must traverse all the hideous tortures of the soul which that lost spirit had learnt in its dire wanderings.

The ghost stood over me, impending like a doom. Then it suddenly looked towards the door, startled, and the door swung on its hinges. A girl entered—a girl dressed in black, her shoulders and bosom gleaming white against the dark attire, a young girl with the heavenliest face on this earth. Casting herself on her knees before the apparition, she raised to that dreadful spectre her countenance transfigured by the ecstasy of a sublime appeal. It was Rosa.

Can I describe what followed? Not adequately, only by imperfect hints. These two faced each other, Rosa and the apparition. She uttered no word. But I, in my stupor, knew that she was interceding with the spectre for my life. Her lovely eyes spoke to it of its old love, its old magnanimity, and in the name of that love and that magnanimity called upon it to renounce the horrible vengeance of which I was the victim.

For long the spectre gazed with stern and formidable impassivity upon the girl. I trembled, all hope and all despair, for the issue. She would not be vanquished. Her love was stronger than its hate; her love knew not the name of fear. For a thousand nights, so it seemed, the two remained thus, at grips, as it were, in a death-struggle. Then with a reluctant gesture of abdication the ghost waved a hand; its terrible features softened into a consent, and slowly it faded away.

As I lay there Rosa bent over me, and put her arms round my neck, and I could feel on my face the caress of her hair, and the warm baptism of her tears—tears of joy.

*　*　*　*　*

I raised her gently. I laid her on the sofa, and with a calm, blissful expectancy awaited the moment when her eyes should open. Ah! I may not set down here the sensation of relief which spread through my being as I realized with every separate brain-cell that I was no longer a victim, the doomed slave of an evil and implacable power, but a free man—free to live, free to love, exempt from the atrocious influences of the nether sphere. I saw that ever since the first encounter in Oxford Street my existence had been under a shadow, dark and malign and always deepening, and that this shadow was now magically dissipated in the exquisite dawn of a new day. And I gave thanks, not only to Fate, but to the divine girl who in one of those inspirations accorded only to genius had conceived the method of my enfranchisement, and so nobly carried it out.

Her eyelids wavered, and she looked at me.

"It is gone?" she murmured.

"Yes," I said, "the curse is lifted."

She smiled, and only our ardent glances spoke.

★ ★ ★ ★ ★

"How came you to think of it?" I asked.

"I was sitting in my room after dinner, thinking and thinking. And suddenly I could see this room, and you, and the spectre, as plainly as I see you now. I felt your terror; I knew every thought that was passing in your brain, the anguish of it! And then, and then, an idea struck me. I had never appealed in vain to Lord Clarenceux in life—why should I not appeal now? I threw a wrap over my shoulders and ran out. I didn't take a cab, I ran—all the way. I scarcely knew what I was doing, only that I had to save you. Oh, Carl, you are free!"

"Through you," I said.

She kissed me, and her kiss had at once the pure passion of a girl and the satisfied solicitude of a mother.

"Take me home!" she whispered.

Outside the hotel an open carriage happened to be standing. I hailed the driver, and we got in. The night was beautifully fine and mild. In the narrow lane of sky left by the high roofs of the street the stars shone and twinkled with what was to me a new meaning. For I was once more in accord with the universe. I and Life were at peace again.

"Don't let us go straight home," said Rosa, as the driver turned towards us for instructions. "It seems to me that a drive through Paris would be very enjoyable to-night."

And so we told the man to proceed along the quays as far as he could, and then through the Champs Elysées to the Bois de Boulogne. The Seine slept by its deserted parapets like a silver snake, and only the low rumble of the steam-car from Versailles disturbed its slumber. The million lights of the gas-lamps, stretching away now and then into the endless vistas of the boulevards, spoke to me of the delicious companionship of humanity, from which I had so nearly been snatched away. And the glorious girl by my side—what of her companionship? Ah, that was more than a companionship; it was a perfect intercourse which we shared. No two human beings ever understood one another more absolutely, more profoundly, than did Rosa and myself, for we had been through the valley and through the flood together. And so it happened that we did not trouble much with conversation. It was our souls, not our mouths which talked—talked softly and mysteriously in the gracious stillness and obscurity of that Paris night. I learnt many things during that drive—the depth of her love, the height of her courage, the ecstasy of her bliss. And she, too, she must have learnt many things from me—the warmth of my gratitude to her, a warmth which was only exceeded by the transcendent fire of my affection.

Presently we had left the borders of the drowsy Seine, which is so busy by day, so strangely silent by night. We crossed the immense Place de la Concorde. Once again we were rolling smoothly along the Champs Elysées. Only a few hours before we had driven through this very avenue, Rosa and I, but with what different feelings from those which possessed us now! How serene and quiet it was! Occasionally a smooth-gliding carriage, or a bicyclist flitting by with a Chinese lantern at the head of his machine—that was all. As we approached the summit of the hill where the Arc de Triomphe is, a new phenomenon awaited us. The moon rose—a lovely azure crescent over the houses, and its faint mild rays were like a benediction upon us. Then we had turned to the left, and were in the Bois de Boulogne. We stopped the carriage under the trees, which met overhead; the delicatest breeze stirred the branches to a crooning murmur. All around was solitude and a sort of hushed expectation. Suddenly Rosa put her hand into mine, and with a simultaneous impulse we got out of the carriage and strolled along a by-path.

"Carl," she said, "I have a secret for you. But you must tell no one." She laughed mischievously.

"What is it?" I answered, calmly smiling.

"It is that I love you," and she buried her face against my shoulder.

"Tell me that again," I said, "and again and again."

And so under the tall rustling trees we exchanged vows—vows made more sacred by the bitterness of our experience. And then at last, much to the driver's satisfaction, we returned to the carriage, and were driven back to the Rue de Rivoli. I gave the man a twenty-franc piece; certainly the hour was unconscionably late.

I bade good night, a reluctant good night, to Rosa at the entrance to her flat.

"Dearest girl," I said, "let us go to England to-morrow. You are almost English, you know; soon you will be the wife of an Englishman, and there is no place like London."

"True," she answered. "There is no place like London. We'll go. The Opéra Comique will manage without me. And I will accept no more engagements for a very, very long time. Money doesn't matter. You have enough, and I—oh, Carl, I've got stacks and piles of it. It's so easy, if you have a certain sort of throat like mine, to make more money than you can spend."

"Yes," I said. "We will have a holiday, after we are married, and that will be in a fortnight's time. We will go to Devonshire, where the heather is. But, my child, you will be wanting to sing again soon. It is your life."

"No," she replied, "you are my life, aren't you?" And, after a pause: "But perhaps singing is part of my life, too. Yes, I shall sing."

Then I left her for that night, and walked slowly back to my hotel.

ALSO AVAILABLE IN THE NONSUCH CLASSICS SERIES

For forthcoming titles and sales information see
www.nonsuch-publishing.com